Broken Pieces

Broken Pieces

A Tale of Hurt, Betrayal, and Everything in Between

Janis Parker Pressley

ShaBazz Enterprise Publishing

CONTENTS

DEDICATION	vi
DISCLAIMER	ix
PROLOUGE	xi

1	SECTION ONE ~ It All Starts Here	1
2	Surprise Surprise!	27
3	Picking The Flowers	40
4	SECTION TWO ~ The Pandemic	48
5	The Dark Cloud	54
6	SECTION THREE ~ Beginning of The End	60
7	House of Cards	70

EPILOGUE	81
ABOUT THE AUTHOR	83

I am very grateful for my friends and family who have supported me the last few years of my life. A special appreciation to my Belize crew sisters Gloria, Lakieta, Dianna, Diletha, Staci, Nikita, Carole & Renee. The words of wisdom and encouragement have inspired me to complete this book. Special thanks to Ashley and for continuing to listen to my crazy stories without judgement. The best is yet to come!

Copyright © 2023 by Janis Parker Pressley

All rights reserved. No part of this book may be reproduced in any manner whatsoever without written permission except in the case of brief quotations embodied in critical articles and reviews.

First Printing, 2023

DISCLAIMER

This is a work of fiction. Unless otherwise indicated, all the names, characters, businesses, places, events, and incidents in this book are either the product of the author's imagination or used in a fictitious manner. Any resemblance to actual persons, living or dead, or actual events is purely coincidental.

PROLOUGE

"Get the fuck out of my house, please."

Mom uttered these words sternly, as though we were completely unrelated.

It was the pinnacle of emotionlessness - if there was a word like that. I felt like I was drowning and there was no one to help save me from the cards I'd been dealt in life. How was this my family? In my mind, at that instant, I felt a door slam shut- blocking me from replaying the feeling of hurt over and over. No one, especially not me, deserved to be treated like dirt by their mother.

I was **D.O.N.E.**

Done with the attitude, arrogance, and drama.

I've had enough of listening to my mother just because she was my mother. Isn't love supposed to be a barometer from the people who claim to care about and adore you? How then could a mother or lover make it a point to only magnify your worst traits? I adored my mother, but there are some things you should never say to someone you love.

Even though I was certain, I still managed to say,

"Is that really what you want? That, I leave?"

In a crystal-clear voice that still rings in my head till today, saying :

"Yes. Get the fuck out, Paula!".

That would be the last thing I ever heard her say.

I drove away, drained and deflated. I had to face the fact that the gaping hole in my heart, needing parental love, might never be filled.

One thing I could have never imagined was that I would hear those exact words three years later. This time, the words would shatter my heart, stinging deeper than my mother's had. And years later, I would

PROLOUGE

still be picking up the broken pieces. Oh, what I would give for the chance to go back in time and swipe down on Brian's profile on Hinge.

1

SECTION ONE ~ It All Starts Here

Butterflies, Butterflies EVERYWHERE

A football addict like Brian would sound weird if he chose a date over a football game.

Even his pals knew better than to disturb him about anything other than the subject on game day, especially when his favorite team was playing.

More often than not, I'd casually strike up a discussion with him to find out what he's up to. Oh my, he made it all seamless.

"Hey, what plans do you have for 3 pm?"

After texting, I said a silent prayer that he wouldn't leave my message unread.

Imagine the huge grin on my face when he responded with:

"UMMMMMM... football... on TV. But if I get a choice between you and football, I am choosing you. What's up?"

Oh yeah! Such a brilliant, enchanting response. I felt like a schoolgirl all over again, all giddy with shivers running down my spine. It took me right back to when we first met...

Paula

It was a beautiful spring day, and the sun was smiling down on us. I closed my eyes as I slowly inhaled the fresh smells of spring - the flowers coming into bloom, the freshly cut grass, and the crisp clean air. Yup, this, officially, was my favorite time of the year. Everything was so fresh, it reminded me of new beginnings, and who didn't love those? I could feel a smile tug at the corners of my lips as I walked from my front door to my car in the driveway. I was on my way to the local market to see what goodies they had. The market was especially vibrant during springtime. There was a lot of great fresh produce to choose from, as well as some truly wonderful homemade stuff. I was going to meet up with one of my friends, Christine, there. Hitting the local market was our thing. We always enjoyed the buzz of people moving from table to table and the delightful smells of food that wafted through the air.

Today was no different. The market was already bustling with people, and my nose caught the delicious smell of samoosas. Boy, did I love those. I always looked forward to having them each time I was at the market. I especially enjoyed the spicy ground beef ones.

"Hey girl!" I hugged Christine when we saw each other.

She looked amazing in her floral patterned dress, and I told her as much.

"Hmmm, not too shabby yourself, " she teased.

"Haha! Thanks." I was wearing a simple pair of jeans and a T-shirt, nothing fancy. I wanted to be as comfortable as possible. I was going to the local market, after all, not the spring ball! I grabbed Christine's hand and started towards the table where they sold samoosas. As we approached, she burst out laughing.

"Of course! Why didn't I guess sooner? You really love your Indian food, don't you?"

"Only because it's the best!" I responded enthusiastically.

I bought a few for us, and we started our walkabout.

"Oh hey Paula, have you seen this year's produce? It looks amazing! Let's head on over there now."

"Sure, lead the way."

She wasn't kidding. The fruits and vegetables looked so good, you could buy them all. Like kids in a toy store, we went about selecting what we wanted. We had to stop ourselves from overdoing it because it would be a waste if we got too much. Satisfied with our purchase, we decided to walk on over to the tables with homemade accessories. A beautiful green scarf immediately caught my attention. I put it on and turned to get Christine's opinion. Instead, I came face-to-face with a not-so-stranger.

So, Brian and I met on Hinge, the dating app, and we'd had great chemistry right off the bat. I definitely enjoyed talking to him; he was so charming. We had finally agreed to see each other in person and not just through a computer screen. We were still working out the details. In a conversation we had yesterday, I had mentioned to Brian that I would be at the market, but I didn't expect him to be there! What a surprise!

"That certainly looks good on you," said a smiling Brian.

Caught off guard, I felt a little flustered, "Oh, th-thanks."

I looked up at him. Oh my. What a handsome man. Was that my heart fluttering? *Oh, come on, Paula!* I quickly reprimanded myself. *The last thing you need right now is another man. You and the girls are doing just great.* The thought of my daughters made me smile.

"And a beautiful smile to match!" The stranger broke into my reverie. My attention came back to him. He was smiling down at me and I noticed a suggestion of a dimple on his right cheek. Dear Lord, he was handsome! The cat suddenly had my tongue. I must have looked as flustered as I felt because his brow creased slightly.

"I'm sorry. I hope I did not offend you in any way."

He went on "I'm so sorry, I didn't let you know who I was. I recognized you immediately but, I suppose I don't look like my photos? I guess... I have catfished you!"

"What? Oh, oh! Not at all. Sorry, I was just..." I paused, "thinking about someone just then."

"Oh. I see." He sounded disappointed. Wait! Did he think that by someone, I meant a special someone? I giggled. That seemed to take him aback a little. He raised an eyebrow.

"Sorry, I seem to be having one conversation with you and another one going on in my head," I explained.

"Really? What's that conversation inside your head?" He folded his arms across his chest.

"Well, it occurred to me that when I said I was thinking of someone just then, you may have thought I was talking about someone special in my life. Well, it's not too far from the truth, just not in that way."

This time he laughed. "Oh yeah? In what way then?"

"I was actually thinking about my daughters."

"Ah! Didn't see that one coming. But I can't say I'm not glad to hear that, because I am." He looked genuinely relieved. He shifted his shoulders as he relaxed slightly. "I'm Brian, by the way."

"Paula," I said as I grinned and accepted his outstretched hand in a handshake. I knew he was doing the whole we've just met act for the sake of my friend. I had been clear that I didn't want anyone in my business. After all, we weren't really an item yet.

His hand felt warm and, oddly, calming.

I turned to Christine and pulled her in. She was standing not too far from us, a broad smile lighting up her face.

"And this is my friend, Christine," I introduced her.

"Nice to meet you, Christine."

"Likewise."

"Well, we had better be going then," I said as I turned to leave.

"Umm, sorry. I hope I'm not being too forward by asking if you would like to join me for a coffee sometime?" he asked.

I was about to politely decline, and Christine must have sensed it because she quickly replied, "She would love to!"

Brian looked at Christine and then to me questioningly. Christine gave me a nudge.

"Ummm, ok. Yeah, I suppose that's ok. Sure."

His face broke into a smile. "Great. Can I get your number so I can send you the details?" We had only been communicating through the app and I had been adamant about not giving him my personal number. Now, with him right here in the flesh, it would be a little awkward if I didn't give it to him.

We exchanged numbers before we said our goodbyes.

"Paula! He is so handsome, oh my word. Ooooh girl, love definitely loves you," Christine said excitedly.

"Love? That's a big word. I've only just met the guy. Besides, I don't think it will go very far. You know I'm not really on the market. I'm happy with my life as it is. This is just something to do until I meet Mr. Right! They say you have to kiss a few toads before you meet your Prince Charming." Christine laughed, "Who's to say you can't find love a second time around? If it finds you, embrace it! Gina and Gaby are old enough; I'm sure you having a man in your life wouldn't be a problem."

"I hear you, girl, but I'm just not in that headspace. At this point, it feels like work and I'm just not ready to put in the work."

" Tell me you at least think he's a looker," she grinned at me.

"Yes, he is, but man shall not live by bread alone," I said like a preacher delivering a sermon.

We both laughed. Christine knew better than to keep pushing the subject, so she let it go - for now.

***

When he said coffee, I expected to meet at a nice cafe, but I wasn't prepared for where I found myself. I was at the entrance of a fancy-looking winery. I walked in like someone who was lost. I asked the hostess if I was in the correct place. When that was confirmed, she asked if I had a reservation. Well, clearly not! I explained that I was meeting a friend here. She asked for the name, and I gave her Brian's.

"Oh, of course." She signaled to one of the waiters. "Please escort the lady to the *cave a vin.*"

What now?

"This way, please ma'am."

Ma'am? I had come out for a coffee, and I had a waiter addressing me as "ma'am" as though I had come to a fancy dinner. He led me past the tables until we got to a little passageway. There he opened a door to the left. It was a private dining room surrounded by expensive-looking bottles of wine. As he opened the door, I immediately saw Brian as he stood to welcome me.

"What is all this? I thought we were meeting for coffee," I asked after we exchanged greetings.

"Well, I wanted to surprise you and I didn't know how you felt about dinner so I went ahead and planned something."

"Well, if you wanted to know how I felt about it, you should have just asked me. That's what most people do."

He sensed the slight irritation in my voice.

"Look, I'm sorry if I've overstepped. I just wanted to do something nice for you."

"I get it and I'm not mad at that. I would have preferred it if you just told me, especially because we are, in actual fact, strangers. I think a coffee at Starbucks would have been more appropriate."

He looked disappointed. I felt bad. The man was trying to be a gentleman and here I was, berating him for surprising me.

"Well, we can think of this as a fancy coffee," I smiled slightly. "It's hard for me to think of it as dinner - it's five. Besides, I'm hardly dressed for the occasion." I was making banter.

"You look absolutely beautiful to me," he said in the way of a compliment.

I had decided to wear a nice semi-casual dress for our coffee meeting. I didn't want to be too casual. Thank goodness I had made that choice.

I wasn't too out of place here. For the first time, I noticed how beautiful the room was that we were in. It was like an elegant wine room with beautiful decor. This must have cost him a bit, I imagined.

He noticed me taking in the room and the surroundings.

"This is called a *Cave a vin*. It's French for a wine room. It is pretty great, isn't it?

"Hmmm, sounds like you are out to impress."

"Are you? Impressed, I mean?"

"Meh," I teased. He laughed.

"Now, before you think I'm this fancy guy, I'm pretty much a regular Joe who just did his homework."

The 'coffee date' went pretty well, and we discovered we had a lot in common and we clearly enjoyed each other's company. The conversation was good and so was the food.

"Well, Mr. Regular Joe, I could get used to this!" We both laughed.

At the end of the evening, we both agreed we'd had a good time, and he asked if he could see me again. I was a bit torn. I really enjoyed tonight and I hadn't really expected to. On the other hand, I didn't want to give him hope of a relationship down the road. He could sense my hesitation.

"Why don't we just meet at a park or something for a stroll as we enjoy the beauty of Spring together? Just two people who enjoy each other's company."

"Ok, I can do that." Put that way, it took a lot of the pressure off.

"Great then, I'll see you Friday?" he asked tentatively.

"Friday's good."

Brian

From the time his eyes popped open, Brian felt that it was going to be a great day. He was finally going to meet the woman he'd been talking to on Hinge for the past few weeks. She had mentioned she was going to be at the Spring market today so he was going to surprise her. He was pretty excited - he felt like a young man again. He could hardly describe how he felt. Perhaps it was the Spring. He enjoyed this season, with its newness. It almost felt like a new beginning. He checked his phone for notifications like he normally did before getting out of bed. There were three messages, one from Shaun and two from Amanda. Oh boy! What did Amanda want? He had made it clear that they weren't dating. They had just been having a good time and that was it. She wanted more from him, but he couldn't give her what she wanted. He was a sworn playa, and settling down was not on the cards for him. He was happy with that; in fact, he preferred it that way. In his opinion, commitment was overrated. He didn't need to settle down with anyone. He read Shaun's message asking him to pick up more beers for the game later. Derek and Josh had decided to join the watch party. Great! The more, the merrier. He wanted to ignore Amanda's messages, but his curiosity got the better of him. She was trying to see him so they could talk.

"Girl, bye," he said as he put his phone away. He wasn't going to respond. She'd get the message.

Without another thought about Amanda, he got ready to go out to the local market. They usually had his friends' favorite beers, and he was looking forward to getting some of those amazing samoosas.

***

He saw her as he approached the samoosa table as she was leaving. She was with another lady, a friend he guessed. It felt like the air was sucked from his lungs, he could hardly breathe. Is this what they meant when they said someone took your breath away? It had happened to him now, so unexpectedly. No girl had ever taken his breath away. He was mostly impressed by their beauty, but nothing more than just the superficial to make him stay long enough. But this girl was different, he felt it to his very core. He had only caught a glimpse of her, and he felt the magnetic pull. It's as though he were under the spell of her siren song.

Come on, man, get a grip. He berated himself for acting like a school-boy. *You're a grown man, and here you are acting like some lost puppy. Shake it off.*

He shifted slightly. Perhaps he needed some water to clear his head. He had smoked quite a few Cohiba cigars last night. He knew deep down that this was not the cigar buzz/hangover talking. He bought a bottle of water anyway and downed half of it in one gulp. But as expected, it did nothing to shake off that magnetic pull he had towards this woman. As though he was activated in that very moment, he felt himself being drawn to her. He shifted his eyes to see if he could find her. He spotted her on the produce aisle. She was moving toward the accessories. As though they had a will of their own, his legs started walking to where she was. He found himself standing beside her as she put on the green scarf she'd been eyeing. His eyes lingered on her, mesmerized by how beautiful she was up close and in person. Her friend seemed to have noticed what was going on because she took a step back and watched, as though a movie was playing right in front of her.

"It looks good on you," he said in the way of a compliment. *Really, man. You couldn't come up with a better opening line? You do this all the time. What's wrong with you today?*

He registered the confused and questioning look on her face. He suddenly felt protective of her. He wanted to reach out and put his hand on her arm to reassure her, but of course that was the last thing he should do. That would be invading her personal space and all sorts of harassment. Despite her flustered look, she smiled. It's as if, with that smile, she tugged at his heartstrings. Right at that moment, he knew an angel was standing before him. She was beautiful, gorgeous, and simply out of this world. He had to say something otherwise he'd be picking his jaw off the ground.

"And a beautiful smile to match!"

"Oh, I was just thinking of someone just then," she said.

He felt as if someone was ripping his heart out of him, as though he was being deprived of air. Of course, she was probably spoken for. She was a devastatingly beautiful woman after all.

Then she giggled, music to his ears. She seemed to be enjoying whatever was going on. She went on to explain that she was thinking about her kids. Boy, he was relieved! So there was no man in her life at the moment,? She would have said something if there was, right? This made him smile on the inside and outside. *She's the one.* Wow! Wait, what? Where did that come from? But he knew it was from a deep place within and it was undeniable, that feeling. The part of him that he couldn't hide from. As he stood staring at this absolute vision of a woman, he knew without a shadow of a doubt that he was going to marry her. When he realized this truth, it was like the window to his heart was open to let in light and air. It had been shut tight for what felt like a hundred years, and this woman, this queen, came and effortlessly opened it. He felt a strong sense of admiration. He went to introduce himself as Brian from *Hinge* and asked her out for coffee and when she hesitated, he sent a silent prayer to heaven for a yes. Prayer answered. Her friend, bless her heart, had accepted the invitation for her. They exchanged numbers, and she left with her friend shortly after. Paula. She had introduced herself as Paula. She had introduced her friend too, but he hadn't even heard her friend's name. He had been polite to her, sure, but his mind was squarely on Paula. She was all that mattered.

***

"Man, since when have you forgotten the beers for your boys and the game? Your bar is ALWAYS stocked to the brim! What happened to you today?" Shaun asked, surprised at Brian's demeanor. He had this quiet pensiveness to him. It was as though something in him had changed.

"Hey, man. Are you ok?"

"Yeah, yeah, yeah. I'm good, man. I think that hangover from too many Cohiba's at last night's bender got me real good."

"Nah, I've seen you with a cigar hangover. This is no hangover. Talk to me man, what's going on?"

Brian just quietly shook his head. He was trying to make sense of it all too. He had so many questions about what happened to him. The sworn playa had met the woman he was going to marry. That made no sense to him. He didn't believe in the commitment thing, didn't care for it. But today, his heart had committed to a perfect stranger, a perfectly beautiful stranger. It was mind-boggling. How could this happen? Not that he was complaining. It took him all by surprise. How could a stranger steal his heart like this?

"My heart's gone, Shaun," he blurted out.

"Huh!" Shaun was clearly confused. "Yeah, I think those cigars did a number on you. Were they the ones you got in Cuba? They may be laced with something..."

"I'm serious Shaun. It's gone."

"I hope you realize that you're not making any sense right now."

Brian sighed resignedly. "Yeah, I know."

"What's going on with you Brian? Derek and Josh are going to be here for the game in no time, you'd better start talking."

"Never mind the game. My head is not in it right now."

Shaun jumped out of his seat.

"Who are you, and what have you done with Brian?"

"Seriously Shaun. My head is out of the game."

"Ooooh, this is major. Game day is your day and you live for them. What has taken my man Brian out of the game?"

"It's a woman."

"Wait, what?! A woman's got you this wound up? Who is this woman and what has she done to you?"

"Her name is Paula. She stole my heart. I met her on Hinge and we met for the first time in person, at the local market when I went to pick up the beers for y'all. From the moment I saw her, I knew she was going to be my wife."

Shaun ran out of the house and back in again. Dramatic.

"Whaaaaaat! Brian talking about marriage? Again, who are you, and where's Brian?"

"I know it sounds crazy, but it's true. She's the one.

Shaun was clearly shocked and still trying to process what he was hearing.

"She must be some woman to make the great playa Brian talk commitment. I have got to meet this miracle worker. Where do you know her from?"

"That's the thing. I don't. I met her on Hinge and in person for the first time at the market. She mentioned she was going and I kinda just showed up and she was there!"

Shaun was even more stunned. "I never thought I'd live to see the day."

"You and me, both."

They sat for a moment in silence. Saying it out loud sounded different than it had in his head. Saying it out loud made it real. Brian the playa had been tamed.

**

He knew from the moment that he laid eyes on her that a coffee date would not be his best foot forward. He had to make a grand gesture. He spent that week thinking about what a romantic date would look like. He dug his heels into it and, so far, he was winning. He thought about calling her to ask her out to dinner instead, but he decided to make it a surprise. He scheduled a date at his favorite winery that had a private dining room. Pleased with himself, he managed to get a reservation. He would spare no expense for the woman of his dreams. On the day of, he decided not to dress to the nines. She was coming in thinking they were having a late coffee, so she'd probably be more casual. He didn't want her to feel out of place or ambushed. And of course, she looked absolutely amazing in her semi-casual dress. But she also looked unimpressed as she walked through the door of the private dining room. She was. She made it clear that she would have preferred if he'd told her beforehand what he was planning. *You blew it, Brian.* His heart sank. So much for trying to be romantic and spontaneous. She probably thought he was a loser now. But he was pleasantly surprised when her demeanor changed.

She teased him about this being "a fancy coffee meeting". Phew! He was still in the game. They went on to enjoy a lovely dinner. If he was being honest, he couldn't remember anything about the food because she was such great company. He felt completely relaxed and like himself. They had a lot in common and they both seemed to want the same things in life. A match made in heaven if you asked him. He couldn't believe just how much he had enjoyed the evening. She was beautiful, smart, and witty.

A Blossoming Romance

Is this normal playa behavior or was it simply his gentle, kind, and a tad-bit mischievous nature at play? I hoped he was the latter because if he's the former, it would hurt deeply to have fallen for a playa. I smiled as I read the sweet message he had just sent. Over the number of dates we had, Brian had opened up about being a playa and how that had all changed when he laid eyes on me. It made me feel special, but, at the same time, I was concerned about his past. Despite my not wanting to be in a relationship from the start, I was falling hard for this charming man. I had no reason to doubt what he said about being a reformed playa. He was as into me as I was into him. A relationship was inevitable.

We've all heard the advice to enjoy the present and take things slowly in life. Well, my new normal consisted of me lingering on the memories of the day, blushing over his texts as I navigated work, whistling and giggling as I got ready for the next day and tucking myself into bed. It was official, Paula was in love!

I wasn't just some middle-aged woman in love... I was a woman whose rough-edged heart had softened in the presence of a real and devoted man. With every day that passed, our love grew stronger. It was almost unbelievable.

Brian was a breath of fresh air, in terms of family and friendship. His soothing words were like a vote of confidence for me and all I stood for. It felt like my heart was being pampered and handled like glass. Oh, how I had longed for this! Growing up, I never had this, and although I learned to shake off my need for love and validation, the little girl in me still needed it and was glad to have Brian treat her lovingly.

Throwback

I was 27 years old when I met him. I had stars in my eyes and ate up what he told me - hook, line, and sinker. I was a woman in love. Craig was my world. He was the first person on my mind when I woke up and the last person I thought about before going to bed. Cheesy, huh? But I felt all those things with Craig. He had promised me the world, and I believed him. Not long after we met, he had asked me to marry him. I was beside myself. We had our first child, Greg, and were married eight years later. I found out I was pregnant with Gina a couple of months after the wedding. My life seemed to be going so well. I was a happily married woman with a husband who adored me. When Gina was 6 months old, I found out I was expecting another baby. I have always worked and had a good job that paid me well. I was a hard worker and continued to climb the career ladder and the salary and perks got better the higher I went. Craig announced that he wanted to start a church. I was excited for him and told him I'd help to hold down the fort while he worked to build the ministry.

All seemed to be going great, so when we found out we were expecting Gaby, I was beside myself. Four months before I had Gina, I got a new job managing a million dollar non profit. They knew I had two kids, Greg and Gina. No one knew that I was pregnant again with the third, except my boss. She came to town to attend my annual awards fundraising gala. Since she arrived the day before, I agreed to take her to dinner and then to her hotel. As we sat at dinner, I had a sudden urge to go to the restroom. As soon as I stood up, I felt water running down my leg as if I had gone to the bathroom on myself. I rushed to the bathroom and the water didn't stop. My water had broken and I was in labor four months early!

I was so embarrassed. I was at dinner with my boss and I had gone into labor! I cleaned up as best as I could and walked back to our table to let my boss know what was happening. She remained calm and asked if we needed to call an ambulance. She asked if I could call Craig and find out the location of the nearest hospital. He immediately made arrangements for Gina and Greg to go to my brother's house while my boss drove me to the hospital that Craig had directed us to. Fortunately, it was only a 10-minute ride from the restaurant to the hospital. Craig was going to meet us there. My boss dropped me off at the hospital entrance while she parked the Suburban. To her, driving that Suburban felt like she was driving a semi-truck.

This was the same hospital where I had delivered Gina, just 10 months before. This was also where my doctor's office was. I had been here over 50 times, but for some reason, I got lost. I spent the next 15 minutes wandering the secluded dark hallways trying to find the labor and delivery area. Each turn I made led to a dead end, and I started to have a panic attack. Clearly, I was lost, all I could think about was having my baby in the cold, bland hallways of this hospital. Determined to make it out, I closed my eyes, said a prayer, and not so long afterwards, as I wandered the hallway, I heard a familiar voice in the distance. It was my boss! She was having a conversation with the labor and delivery nurses, asking them where I was. The staff on duty repeatedly said, "Ma'am, there is no one here by the name of Paula. In fact, we have not had anyone by that name all day."

My boss became even more frustrated, "Well, that can't be right. I just dropped her off myself at the hospital entrance about 15 minutes ago, and I saw her enter the building. So, unless you're telling me she's disappeared or been kidnapped, I'm sure that she's in here somewhere."

It was at that point when my boss's voice got louder that I was close enough to get her attention and respond, "Here I am."

She breathed a sigh of relief. "Where on earth had you gone?" she asked, concerned.

I was a 38-year-old in labor at 28 weeks of pregnancy. A geriatric mother giving birth for the third time and in full-blown labor. The nurses immediately took me to a room and called my doctor. They gave me drugs to stop the labor and put a monitor on me to make sure my baby was not in distress. Within 15 minutes, my doctor was in my room.

Dr. J said, "Paula, I have good news and bad news. The good news is that you will be a mom in the next 24 hours, otherwise, you would remain in the hospital for the next 6 weeks. The bad news is that tomorrow morning I'm going on vacation, and if you have the baby in the next 24 hours, I won't be here for the delivery as my plane leaves at 9 A.M. I will consult with my partner Dr. K, and he will take good care of you. In fact, I've asked him to meet me here tonight so I can do the proper introductions."

Crazy thoughts started whirling in my mind. *What in the entire hell! I'm in labor and Dr. J, the person who I trusted for the last 2 years to deliver Gina, and now he won't be here for this new baby when I need him most. Now I have to open up my legs to a total stranger, someone that I don't even know! I just want to go back home to the way it all was before this crazy evening.*

Tears started streaming down my face. I was feeling abandoned and alone in this extremely vulnerable moment. Dr. J put a firm hand on my shoulder.

"I'm sorry, Paula. I know you must be feeling a lot of things right now. But everything is going to be alright."

Oh, he had no idea!

At that moment, Dr. K walked in. Dr. J introduced us and handed over my case to his colleague.

"Paula, you are in good hands. I want you to relax and allow Dr. K to take care of you. Can you do that?"

I nodded, reluctantly. I resigned myself to the fact that Dr. K, who I had just met a second ago, was going to be my attending doctor.

By the time I was done with my pity party, my husband Craig had made it to the hospital. He, too, was kind of upset because he was scheduled to interview for a new job at 10 A.M. the next morning. He was nervous and had driven like a bat out of hell to get the other kids up and out of their beds, to my brother's house, for safekeeping.

At this point, it was just a waiting game, and while I had been induced and had gone through long labors with Greg and Gina in excess of 24 hours, it was evident that this baby was coming sooner rather than later.

Dr. K asked them to give me something for my baby's lungs and to monitor the dilation of my cervix. By midnight I was in full sleep mode though I was having mild contractions. By 5 A.M., the nurses told me I should get an epidural because it was time. This little baby was ready, and I needed to be ready too.

They had me bend over the side of the bed, with my back arched, and head down. The epidural was in and they were preparing to welcome this premature baby into the world. They placed my feet in the stirrups and asked me to give one big push, which I did. This baby was so small that with one push, she popped out. Dr. K and the nurses shouted for me to stop pushing. My baby was here and there was complete silence. I didn't see or hear her. She was breathing so they put her in an incubator and whisked her away. As she was being wheeled off, I heard a faint sound- a whimpering, almost like a puppy in distress. There was no yelling or screaming like I had experienced with the last two.

An hour later, my boss showed up in my room. "Paula, my goodness, you did really well. I just saw your little angel in the NICU. What a miracle!" she exclaimed. "How are you feeling?"

"Honestly, this was unlike the births of the other two, and I don't feel like I have actually given birth. It's all so surreal and unbelievable."

I had given birth to a one-pound baby girl who was smaller than the size of my hand. She looked like a little doll hooked up to all those machines.

After the doctors examined her, it was determined that she had no health issues and she was perfect in every way. What a relief! She would, however, remain in the NICU for monitoring, feeding, and growth for the next several weeks.

The hardest part was the day of my delivery. I was missing the most important night of the year for my job - our annual fundraiser. My boss had to attend the event alone, and most attendees, including my Board of Directors, were very curious about why I wasn't there. Truth is, I was in the hospital, and no one on my staff or the board even knew that I was expecting a baby. I just hadn't told them yet. I knew that most of them would have some concerns and questioned the fact that baby Gina was not even a year old.

The nursing staff took me to the NICU a few times, and this place was different. Lights and sirens were constantly going off to send alerts that something was wrong. My baby had tubes everywhere and was blindfolded. She looked like a small alien creature, not a newborn baby. When I looked at her, all I could do was cry and wonder what I did wrong to be dealt this set of cards.

I knew a couple of friends who had premature children, mostly boys, and I wondered if my daughter would experience any of the same issues as they had. I was assured that the chances of survival for black female premature babies are the best for all preemies. That alone gave me some confidence and comfort that my baby would be ok.

The day after Gaby was born, the nursing staff started talking about discharging me from the hospital. I never imagined what it would be like to leave the hospital without my baby. I had carried her inside of me for 28 weeks. The emptiness I felt on the inside, knowing that I would have to show up every day to visit her was overwhelming. Because of how small she was, I was afraid to touch her for fear of breaking her bones, which were still very fragile. All I could do was watch her sleep in the incubator. I was discharged from the hospital the day after I gave birth to Gaby and started coming in every day to see her.

I must have had a nervous breakdown, and the strain of going to watch my baby sleep, the baby that I couldn't touch, was unbearable. I, in every sense of the word, was a nervous wreck. Every phone call from the hospital in the middle of the night had me on edge. With each call, I was afraid they would tell me that something happened to my baby. Each phone call had me on edge and so nervous that two weeks in, we requested no phone calls unless it was an emergency or calls to let us know she was ok. This helped, but I was still anxious. I asked my boss if I could come back to work so that I wouldn't lose my mind, and she agreed as long as I got permission from Dr. J.

Fortunately, Dr. J had been with me for two years, and he knew that I was having problems staying at home and being away from my baby. He agreed that I could go back to work and take my maternity leave when baby Gaby came home. I was relieved and ecstatic. I got to go back to the job I loved and I would be off when my baby would be coming home for my maternity leave. Relief was right on time.

I went back like nothing had happened and resumed my work. My boss had told my colleagues that I was off sick for the duration of my absence. No one knew that I had just had a baby who was, at that moment, in an incubator. It was my news to tell, and I would tell it when I was good and ready. I didn't immediately say anything because I wanted work to be a distraction from my reality and I didn't feel like talking about it. I became so involved in my work, it gave me the solace that I needed at that time. My boss always kept an eye on me to make sure I wasn't overextending myself. But to my fellow workmates, I was just being hardworking Paula. I would be in the office by 7 A.M. and out at 5 P.M. to go and visit Gina in the hospital. Each time I saw her, my heart would sink. I never quite knew whether she was making any progress or not. The NICU nurses always assured me that she was doing really well. I guess I wanted to see her open her eyes and wrap her tiny little hand around my finger.

***

It was eight more weeks before they could clear Gina to come home. When we got the call, I was in the kitchen, whipping up sandwiches for Craig and the kids. The phone rang, and I picked it up after a few rings, annoyed that Craig hadn't made an effort to get it. He was glued to his computer screen, working on a sermon for this Sunday.

"Yes?" I must have sounded as irritated as I felt because the person on the other end seemed to pick up on it.

"I'm really sorry to disturb you. I'm calling from the hospital, and I wanted to find out if you could come in this afternoon."

Badaboom! My heart did a number. Was something wrong with Gina? I started shaking.

"Is everything ok?" I asked shakily.

"Oh! Yes, everything is fine. I'm sorry to have alarmed you. The doctor would like to discuss next steps with you."

"Oh!" I heaved a sigh of relief. "Sure, we'll be there."

We put Greg and Gaby into the car and drove to my brother's to drop them off so we could get to the hospital. Thankfully, my brother was ok to watch the kids for a few hours while we were at the hospital. Bless his heart, he had been a real help with them while we navigated the last few weeks of our lives. When we got there, Gina's doctor saw us immediately.

"I have some really great news for you. Gina is now cleared to go home. She's really thriving and we see no need to keep her here any longer."

I could kiss him right now! I was so excited to hear that we could finally take baby Gina home to meet her brother and sister. She could finally be home with us, where she belonged! And with that, a weight felt like it had been lifted off my shoulders.

***

For the next few weeks, we struggled, hell, I struggled. My non-profit only paid half the salary for maternity leave, and by this time, Craig had quit his job to do ministry full time. The truth was that the ministry did not pay a salary and we had 3 kids at home and two under two years old. When Gaby was 2 weeks old, I went back to work. I could not afford to be on maternity leave while my child was in the NICU fighting for her life, with me watching over her in the incubator because I couldn't even touch her.

When I initially told Craig I was going back to work, I was taken aback when he said I couldn't do that. How would we pay the bills if I didn't? I had asked him to get part-time work while he worked at the church to pay the bills. He argued that his schedule was jam-packed and he couldn't possibly work, counsel the sheep, and study for sermons; and he was nearly getting his Ph.D. I worked until my ninth month of pregnancy and only took the 2-week maternity leave they gave me. It was hard leaving Gaby when she was that small, but I had to. Someone had to make the money. Finally, Craig started doing ministry full time and I was thrilled for him. I thought he'd get straight to looking for a job, but he said he needed time to blow off some steam. I understood and left that alone. Weeks turned into months, and months rolled into years. Craig was in no hurry to get to work. He was content and settled into becoming a stay-at-home dad and full time Minister, something that was never discussed.

I started feeling the weight of being the involuntary sole bread-winner of the family. After a while, I was done. I couldn't put up with the bum that Craig had become, so I filed for divorce. I had loved Craig deeply, and I knew he loved me too, but his unwillingness to pull his weight broke us. So I knew from then that it was nice to have love, but you needed more than love to make a relationship work. Craig and I were not on the same page when it came to work ethic and sharing responsibility. He had been more than happy to dump that all on me. Years later, after personal counseling, he said thank you. He thanked me for everything I'd given him, then he said he was sorry for not being the husband that I deserved. That gave me the closure I needed. I carried this lesson on love ever since, and now that Brian was in the picture, I wanted to make sure that he was responsible and that our values aligned. It all seemed to fall into place.

I Called Her Mother

My mother, in her younger years, had been an athlete- she moved faster than the speed of light. For about 25 years post-retirement, she walked daily. My mom was never absent, but neither was she present. There were many things about her that I only got to know in the latter part of her life, and I guess that was what made her the cold, unfeeling woman I had grown up with.

Unfortunately, as she got older, basic things like walking and talking became an issue for her after suffering a couple of strokes. She no longer wanted to take pictures because she was concerned about the way her face looked. *Let's talk about being vain.*

We were given very explicit instructions on what to do and not to do at her time of death.

"No open caskets. Cremate me, and put a nice picture up for people to see."

I got a call from my sister, during the early period of seeing Brian, saying that my mom had fallen face forward and was in the ER with a huge gash to her forehead. She had an encounter with a tree stump that left her face down in the dirt. My sister was unable to get her up, so an ambulance had to be called.

Other than the scar, the fall had no impact on my mom. She still felt nothing inside. The inability to feel isn't just about physical feeling; it's also about words that come out of your mouth. And because of this, her piercing, injurious words didn't shake her one bit. Words matter; how *you say things* matter.

The human mind can only take so much. There's a limit to how much you can sit down and endure when parents repeatedly say negative things over and over to you.

"You are too pretty to be so fat"

"You are so skinny...you look anorexic".

"Are you going to eat all that?!!!"

"Look at your kids, they are going to be fat, just like you."

It was typical of mom to let out a comment on everything. Sadly, her words were often cold and heartbreaking, like a dagger through my soul.

Each time those kinds of words came out of my mother's mouth, they stung like acid and pushed me further, into the depths of despair. People say depression is real and can interfere with one's self-esteem. However, over my life, I stopped looking for compliments as any congratulations were always met with another statement to make sure I was knocked back down a peg or two. Always comparing, always being negative, and always critical of anything I did- and angry because I didn't let her control my life and tell me what to do.

I cannot possibly compare Brian with my mom. Not even close. They brought me pain on different levels. But as I admitted, Brian was a breath of fresh air when we met. He was like cold water on a scorching day, with weather of 70 degrees. I gulped him down like a woman who was starved for love- because although it's painful to admit this, at the time, I was.

Love

Love is beautiful, forgiving, dynamic, not envious, not selfish. Brian was altruistic, and this quality made me love him to no end. He was so gracious, attentive to the minute details, and it's safe to say he swept me off my feet. He made me feel so safe, so secure in his love. He often told me about how he'd known from the first time he laid his eyes on me that he was going to marry me. He often described it as an awakening deep within him.

Love was our propelling force, and we took off on it. The extent of our love for one another was evident to my family and friends, who respected him enough not to base their opinion of him solely on his appearance or past. I mention his appearance because while I always dressed the part, Brian was more comfortable wearing a pair of jeans and a throwback jersey. But I saw past all that. Love was not superficial. I stayed true to myself and my belief that love went beyond feeling and looks. It was about supporting each other and standing in each other's corner. And he did all that. He showed me time and again the love that I craved and deserved. If there had been a love meter or some other means to gauge our chemistry, it would have always remained green. This love we had…; it was life-giving. It made me glow.

Trust

Trust is earned, not something you ask for on a silver platter. Brick by brick, trust is built through a process that takes time. For someone who has had numerous girlfriends, there was not the slightest bit of dread or uncertainty about the personality he showed to me. It seemed too genuine to be true at first, but as time passed, I gradually began to trust him, though in the back of my mind, I seemed to wait for the other shoe to drop. Craig had done that. I fell in love with him, and he'd let me down. But again, Brian gave me no reason to believe he was that person.

Perfect love drives out fear, right? Trust was made simpler by Brian than I could have ever imagined. I always knew where he was, at all times. There was no sneaking around.

He was charming and very consistent. You could set a clock by his actions. Always up at 4 am, out the door by 5:00 am, at work at 6:30 am, lunch at 11:30 am, leaving work at 3:30 pm, and home by 5:30 pm every Monday through Friday. Never missed a day of work, very consistent in everything he did.

At that point in my life, I felt that was the level of consistency I needed to get my life running well too. In all honesty, he challenged me to be stable for myself, my kids, and all other things I was involved in. Gradually, the thought of having a stable and consistent man as a husband would creep into my thoughts. Sometimes I tried to distract myself from being too forward with this guy who brightened up my day. Other times, I would just allow myself to live in the moment. We connected in so many ways.

Why spoil good moments with a good man because of thoughts that made my heart race- *not in a good way*?

Will A Playa Always Be A Playa?

"Vet him very well."
"You sure he isn't just pretending?"
"Your man is quite solid and social."
"Heard anything about his romantic escapades?"
My heart would skip a beat whenever these questions were thrown at me. I felt haunted. The life of a player is quite unpredictable. Was he being honest with me? I had met him on a dating site after all, so who knew? But I had immediately been captivated by his easy-going nature, his love, and his care. He reassured me that he was the real deal. How we met was beside the point. It didn't hurt that he looked good too! He always wanted to meet all of my friends and family, both near and far and was always generous. He always paid for everything when we were out, even with friends - food, drinks, gifts, you name it. He even purchased Christmas gifts for my girlfriends (prior to this, I had not been getting gifts for either them or their husbands, to be honest!)

"Paula, fear and love do not go hand in hand," I would say, speaking ever-so-softly, to myself.

The same people who asked questions took their time to do the vetting. No concerns at all, ever. This made it the second reason he was a miracle. My miracle. A playa who becomes transparent and consistent is worth more than gold. I even had him vetted by ALL my close friends, family members, and most importantly, my children. They said how much they liked him and saw him as a father figure. That was just what I wanted to hear. A man who loved me and my kids was worth holding onto. Everyone said he was great, and our life together would be amazing. This time, not a tiny bit of nagging fear remained.

Our amazing life became official when we went for an evening stroll. He became *my* man. To me and all who cared about me, this was all that mattered.

The present.

2

Surprise Surprise!

The Proposal that had Everyone Talking

We started out just like any other Saturday, running errands. Brian stated he wanted to visit the tuxedo shop to try on a tux for an upcoming event and then wanted to meet friends for lunch at a golf country club. An afternoon that was meant to be simple became a story I was willing to share and tell anyone who cared enough to ask or give a moment to listen. We had cultivated the habit of having our *"us-time"* regardless of our busy schedules. Over time, I learned that it takes a certain level of intentionality to create time to show loved ones how much they mean to us.

Brian was the man, especially when it came to creating time for those he loved. That whole process made me appreciate the essence of love and light. When love steps in, light paves the way, light shines on the path and love seems to expound. This is the perfect description, theorized from our experience. There was so much love we showed and shared, and I, of course, had enough light to lead me each step of the way. But still, fear had to be crushed. My fear of "Do I deserve this overwhelming happiness?"

Loving a single mother came with its baggage. My kids were foremost on my mind - it didn't matter that they were no longer babies. It was a no-brainer: whoever I'd be with had to be comfortable with who I was, the mother I *am*. I wanted my girls to be comfortable with him too. I just wanted to love and be loved, not managed or pitied. I wasn't even doing badly on my own, so why worry about desperation to be with a man when I had not been lonely before he came into my life ? This was my thought process all along, before Brian swept me off my feet.

I never really thought I'd have my second attempt at a love that was oh-so-beautiful. I mean, when you get to a certain stage in life, you become comfortable with where you're at and change can be really scary. As I said, I was good, pretty much set in my ways. So why was I on a dating site? Well...

Hinge

"Mom, you've got to do this! It's been a gazillion years since you've had someone. You need someone who'll be there for you, for a change," that was Gina.

"Yeah, Mom," Gaby agreed.

I rolled my eyes as I laughed, "I'll get someone when you both get someone."

Gina laughed, "Then you'll be waiting awhhhiiile!"

We all laughed.

"But seriously Mom, have you ever thought about having someone since Dad?"

"Honestly, at some point I did, but I guess I just never got around to doing it. I kept telling myself I would, and here we are."

You see, when I left Craig, I became laser focused on my career, and it paid off in dividends. I had managed to create the life that I wanted, albeit the fact my husband and father of my children was no longer in it. I had been afraid that being a single mom was going to be really tough, but it wasn't as bad as I had thought it would be. Now, don't get me wrong, being a single mom is no walk in the park, but I guess I was one of the lucky ones who didn't have to struggle as much. My girls were in school and I lined up extra-curricular activities for them, which they both loved. Gina enjoyed her ballet classes, she was always dancing around the house. Gaby had developed a passion for music, so I enrolled her in music classes, and she did really well. I consider myself blessed to have been able to give my girls all these things. I was able to spend weekends with them, when they were not spending it at their dad's. So it worked out pretty well for us. Of course, I had the support of my wonderful family and friends who cheered me on. I thank God for such blessings!

"The more reason for you to do this then...for you," Gaby's voice broke into my reverie.

"Hmmm...we'll see."

"No Mom. Now."

"I don't know sweetheart. These dating sites are more your generation than mine. In my time, you met a good man in church or in a decent place like work. Now, anyone can say they're Superman online and who's to say they aren't? They all lie and say things that don't really represent them - fly fishing I think it's called? How do you know who to trust? How many toads and lizards do you have to kiss before finding a genuine person? Besides, what would my friends say if they heard I'm on a dating site? As I said, I'm from a different time. "

"Mom, I get your point and I agree that people are fake out there. And by the way, it's catfishing. But even if you were to meet a guy, say in church, how do you know that he's got good intentions? What if he's a loser like the guy from the bar or the funny dating site? You can't vouch for someone just because you met them in a "respectable" place. Some men's hearts are desperately wicked, Mom. And about your friends, you don't have to tell them if you don't want to. See how it goes first and if you want to, you can tell them later on."

I looked at Gaby, a smile beaming on my face, "Girl, whoever raised you did it right. Look at the good head that's on your shoulders."

Gaby giggled.

"Well, I got it from my mama!" she said as she came in for a hug.

"Okay. Let's see how this world of online dating works, and I say this with some reluctance. I can't promise I will take it as seriously. I hardly even check my Facebook, let alone a dating app. It just sounds like work."

"Mom, don't worry. We'll get you all set up and ready to go. All you have to do is respond to any messages or notifications, and that's it! Easy peasy, lemon squeezy."

"For you, maybe. Let's see."

In no time, my girls had me set up on Hinge. At first, I agreed so that they could see that I was trying (though I really wasn't. It was all up in the air at that point).

I soon forgot about Hinge and went about my life as usual. Then I got an 'interested' notification from some guy named Brian. I mean, I had been getting them since I'd joined but I had quickly realized that some of these dudes were fake and just mucking around. If it walks like a duck! I'd get dudes who were young enough to be my nephew pinging me, it was ridiculous. The first few guys I'd responded to had quickly turned the conversation to sexual stuff, so I knew that they were just in it for all the wrong reasons. Eventually, I had just laughed it off and thought how right I had been in my reluctance to sign up for these things. But when Brian pinged me, I was surprised to see the face of a middle-aged man staring back at me. It wasn't any of those fresh-faced young men that had flooded my notifications. But in the back of my mind, I was thinking *why would a middle aged-man be on a dating site? Shouldn't he be home with his wife and kids?* Then I got a mental check. *Yeah, and I bet he's also wondering the same about you. You don't even know the man. If you are going to pass judgment, at least get to know him a little first.* And with that, I had responded to him.

It started off with friendly chatter and light stuff, like, "Hey, how was your day?" to asking each other questions about ourselves until, before I knew it, we were talking really freely with each other. I often found myself looking forward to our chats. Our conversations were so effortless and meaningful. I constantly cautioned myself that the reason it flowed was because we were hiding behind our phone screens.. I would sometimes wonder if it would all fall apart, like a house of cards, if we were to do this in person. Then he asked if we could meet. At first, I wasn't sure if it was a good idea. What if it turned out that I was being catfished? I had been worried about that too the whole time we chatted. Was this guy just saying things he thought I wanted to hear? Was he just some bored dude whiling away the time by chatting to me, or was he a scammer who would eventually try to fleece me of my hard-earned money? I knew I had to be careful and take everything with a pinch of salt. So you can understand my reticence in meeting the guy in person. I'd told him I was going to think about it, but a week went by and I didn't say anything about the matter until he slid it into a conversation we were having.

"You know, I'm still waiting to hear from you about meeting up in person. And I get that you might be concerned about whether this is even real and if I'm being for real. But all I can do is give you my word, whatever it's worth to you, that I'm one hundred percent real. I have never opened up to anyone the way I've opened up to you. I feel really comfortable talking to you. How about we have a low-key coffee this coming Saturday?"

So he had picked up on my reservations. I was still on the fence.

"I don't know, Brian. It's all so much right now. The thing is, my friends don't know I'm on a dating site, much less that I was having deep, meaningful conversations with someone on it. Besides, I'll be meeting with a friend for the Spring market on Saturday."

Christine was one of my most trusted friends, and she had some pretty solid values. I loved that woman because she was a straight-talker, and cared deeply about people. She was the person you would call when you're in trouble, and she'd be right there with you. So now, I wasn't sure how she would react to me being on Hinge and starting to get serious with somebody.

I Didn't See It Coming

It was like any other weekday, ordinary and filled with the usual busyness. I was excited about the upcoming luncheon at the golf country club. It would give me enough time to spend with my girl-friends. I felt like with this whirlwind romance sweeping me up, I could use some girl time, you know, to ground me a little. I swear, this feeling was the stuff of fairy tales. I occasionally pinched myself to make sure I wasn't dreaming. I know! Don't look a gift horse in the mouth, right? I honestly kept waiting for the other shoe to drop, but when it didn't, I was more accepting of my good fortunes. Yes, I was worthy and deserving of love! And here it was, right at my doorstep. The buzz of the alarm on my phone pulled me out of my reverie. Thank goodness; I had left the shower on and forgot to get under it as I was lost in my thoughts. I stepped in and let the warmth of the water soothe and cleanse me. A bath wouldn't be such a bad idea tonight when I got back. Pleased with that thought, I stepped out of the shower and started getting ready for the luncheon.

I stood looking at the clothes I shortlisted for this event. I was caught between my favorite black dress and the green dress Brian had surprised me with. It was a beautiful dress truly fit for a queen. Just looking at it now gave me warm fuzzies. Yup! This was the dress. Such a fitting dress for such a beautiful day. Suddenly, I felt giddy and excited. Wow! Where did that come from? It was probably all these great thoughts of Brian flooding my mind. I honestly thought all this giddiness was for the youngsters. But hey, this man made me feel like I was sweet 16 again, so of course, I was giddy. I started humming a happy tune as I slipped on my green dress. I looked at myself in the full-length mirror - definitely a queen. With a spring in my step, I headed out to the golf country club. I would have gone earlier to help with set-up, but my girlfriends had insisted they had this one covered; something about me always working really hard. I hadn't thought much of it then. They probably really wanted me to take it easy for once and enjoy the luncheon.

I was hoping to see Brian a little later. It was a shame he couldn't make it to this luncheon. Work. This was probably the first luncheon he couldn't attend. Well, at least in this green dress, I wouldn't miss him too much. He would be right there with me. As I pulled into the parking lot, one of my girlfriends approached my car.

"Wow, Paula! You're a vision. We should have sent a limo for you with how good you look."

"Oh, stop," I laughed as I pulled her in for a hug. "But thanks. I feel great."

It was always nice seeing these incredible women I called friends. I started to walk towards the entrance when one of my other girlfriends came flying out to give me a bear hug. "Paula! Oh my! Look at you. Aren't you just a sight for sore eyes?"

"What is this? Flatter Paula day?" I laughed and put an arm around her waist as we walked toward the entrance. If Brian were here, he'd have led the charge in showering me with compliments. It was as if my mind had conjured him up, because there he was, right by the entrance of the country club!

"Brian!" I ran into his arms. A warmth enveloped me as I melted into his embrace.

"You look amazing, baby. You took my breath away," he whispered into my ear.

I didn't know it was possible to melt after you'd already melted. I might as well be a puddle. I was buzzing with the love and warmth that radiated from him. See, this is what I meant when I said Brian was the man when it came to creating time for whomever he loved. And I felt loved in this moment - completely and undoubtedly.

"What are you doing here, babe?" I asked as I gently pried myself from his embrace.

"Ah, well, you know...I missed you, that's all."

"Awww babe, you're so sweet," I gave him a quick peck on the lips. Wouldn't want to cause a scene by recreating a steamy make-out session in front of my girlfriends; no, that wouldn't do.

For the first time, I noticed that he was dressed pretty casually. I frowned slightly,"You going in dressed like that?"

"Oh, I just drove straight from where I was. I didn't have time to change. I've got my tux in the car. I'll change into it now. Just wanted to see you and let you know I was around." He seemed a little nervous. I could see the tiny beads of sweat on his temples.

"Brian are you alright? You seem a little antsy."

"Oh yeah, sure hun. I'm just catching my breath, really. I literally rushed over so I wouldn't miss the luncheon."

I broke into a huge grin as I put my hand to my bosom, clearly touched by his thoughtfulness. "I love you, Brian. Have I ever told you that?"

He seemed to ease up a little at this and smiled widely at me, revealing that cute suggestion of a dimple on his right cheek that I've always adored.

As I turned toward the entrance to suggest that we go in before the luncheon began, I was surprised to see one of my friends with her phone up, grinning from ear to ear. Was she recording us? Why, though? I turned to look at Brian just in time to see him pull out a little black velvet box from the inner pocket of his jacket.

"Wait, what's happening right now?" I was a bit slow on the up-take. A little confused, I looked back at my friend. She was recording. It finally started to sink in.

"Oh my god! Oh my god! OH MY GOD!" Was *this* the proposal? I moved back in disbelief, hands over my mouth.

"What are you doing? Where are you going Paula?" My two girl-friends said.

I hunched over slightly as I felt warm tears trickle down my face.

"Awww, don't cry, " urged one of my friends.

I looked up and Brian was making his way toward me. I could feel my knees shake. I was scared they would buckle and I wouldn't be able to keep standing. This was all so overwhelming...in a good way, though. He dropped down on one knee. d

"Paula, beautiful Miss Paula. Amazing mom, friend, and partner. From the moment I met you, I knew you were the woman for me. You've brought sunshine and so much love and joy into my life. You've made me a better man and have made me want to leave my playa days behind. You are the light that guides me, the air that fills me, and the love that sustains me. And now I'm asking you, wonderful woman, to make me the happiest, most blessed man on this Earth by sharing forever and a day with me. Paula, will you marry me?"

My heart burst open into beautiful warm pink hues. I could feel a warmth travel through my body as though it was a blessing from heaven itself. I could hardly contain myself.

"YES! A thousand times, yes! I'll marry you Brian, of course I will."

The tears were in free fall as he slid the most gorgeous ring onto my finger.

"Woohoo! Woohoo! She said yes!" My friends were cheering us on.

Brian got up from his bended-knee position, looking like he'd just won the lottery. The man was glowing. His grin could not have been wider if he had tried.

He pulled me to him and planted a firm kiss on my lips. Best kiss ever! We embraced, laughing and crying at how beautiful the moment was. I had just agreed to spend the rest of my life with this charming man whose love touched me to the very core. This was my person.

"Congratulations, you two. We are so happy for you. You absolutely deserve this happiness," said one of my friends, who came to hug us both.

Now it all made sense - Brian suddenly showing up even though he had previously said he couldn't make it, his nerves, and the shower of compliments. This was all planned out! Wait, so the luncheon was a decoy to get me to dress up and get to the golf country club! It all made sense why the girls didn't want me to help with setup. There was no set-up!

I couldn't hide the delighted giggle that spontaneously erupted from somewhere deep within me, where joy lived. I felt like a little girl living her fairy tale. With love and admiration in my eyes, I gazed deep into Brian's eyes. He was feeling what I was feeling; I could tell. This was the beginning of happily ever after...or so I thought.

The Celebrity Ring (Good Surprise)

The ring itself was something to behold. Brian had really outdone himself. A five-carat ring. It was breathtakingly gorgeous. As I looked at this beautiful ring, I knew in that moment the value that this man placed on me. I was more than the precious stones and metal that were on my ring finger. He was telling me that I was his everything. I was worth everything to him, and then some. In that moment he was letting me know that he has me, and this was the beginning of something beautiful. When he slipped that ring on my finger, I felt like a queen at her coronation, the crown being placed on her head. I was his queen and this was day one of happily ever after...or was it?

***

Brian's presence and I had gradually adjusted to being with him or him being with the team. I was even more comfortable to know that this man who has finally made up his mind to settle sees who I am and what I do as an interesting part of the life of the woman he goes out with. So, when he finally popped the question, "Will you marry me?" I excitedly said "YES" because he meshed so well into my life.

I said yes to a consistent relationship- to love, to positivity, to building a happy family, to the man who believes in me and my cause, and to a beautiful forever. That magical moment held no iota of doubt, guilt, or displeasure. It was just YES all the way. Whoosh. Magical!

Becoming Mrs. Brian

After we met, Brian started accompanying me to various activities and events. As a member of a sorority, a lot of what we do is volunteering and fundraising. Our second date was to a fashion show fundraiser where I was responsible for managing the silent auction. While he was not there for the set-up, he stayed around and helped me clean up after the event ended. On the third date, we volunteered at a soup kitchen. He got in there as the only man with the group of women and helped us serve food, sort clothes, etc. After that event, he went with a group of us to brunch. He never complained and came to all our events and helped to serve food, sort clothes, and he even donated money. It was like he was a member of the three organizations I was in because of his display of commitment.

We also went to several black-tie formal events. He wore a tuxedo, was in a fashion show fundraiser for breast cancer, and was right by my side in all the things I did. He was even planning on being the President of the Men's group, as it was his goal to get more of the men engaged in what we were doing as women. He spent time meeting with other men asking for their commitment to helping us be more successful. He served as a DJ for a couple of our fundraisers - virtual and in person.

We attended the symphony, opera, weddings, cotillions, fundraisers, and benefit concerts- not just in California but to other states as well. I took him to Memphis a couple of times - including the time we went for my College Homecoming. He was excited about the warm welcome he received because most knew him from the proposal video where he gave me that five-carat ring. It was like he was a celebrity. My personal celebrity!

On one occasion, Shaun had said to me, "I don't know what you've done to Brian but man, he is a different guy. I hardly recognize the dude." He chuckled as he shook his head.

"You sure worked your magic on him."

My heart soared. I felt like I had made him a better man, he even said it quite a few times. I was so happy that I could be this positive influence on him. He was so involved, and his dedication to the things that were important to me was nothing short of astounding.

"Thanks Shaun," I said, "I guess credit also goes to him for being open-minded and open-hearted."

"Yeah, and he got the right person to start him off on this path. He truly is a lucky guy."

"Awww, Shaun. Thanks for saying so. I'm a lucky woman too."

***

At that point, our lives had become so integrated, it already felt like we were a married couple. We were in sync, and we prioritized time spent together no matter how crazy things got. Did we ever have fights? Honestly, not that I recall. Of course, we had little disagreements here and there, but never a blow-up or anything like that. We generally talked things out. Perhaps it's because we were both at a place in our lives where we wanted the same thing, and peace was one of them. We had agreed we didn't want to spend time arguing about silly stuff, and we definitely didn't want to waste time being mad at each other for days on end. We agreed that if either of us felt some type of way about something, we'd talk about it and not let it fester. It did wonders for our communication.

The way I see it is, as you grow older, there are certain things that you don't need in your life, and one of those things is strife. It's true what they say, with age comes wisdom. Don't get me wrong, I wasn't always this way. I was quite the firecracker when provoked, but I realized how much energy and joy it took away from me, so I decided it wasn't worth it. Where I would get mad if someone cut in front of me, I now choose to let it go. So when Brian came into my life, I was pleased to find that he mirrored me in that aspect. We had both made personal decisions to live happier lives. The fruit of that showed. To those who knew us, we were the golden couple. Even my daughters were really pleased for me. They'd tease me about how I'd been adamant about not joining a dating site.

"Aren't you glad you did it now?!"

"Yeah, yeah. I guess you were right. But don't forget all those crazy ones before Brian came along. Boy was it exhausting!"

"Wasn't it you who talked about kissing a few toads, before getting to Mr. Right?"

We laughed. But I was grateful that my girls could see me this happy at this stage of my life.

I was content. I was at peace. I was loved. I was cared for. I mattered to someone. I was someone's world. I had it all.

3

Picking The Flowers

The Kryptonite Wedding

Flowers were neatly arranged in pews and rows. All pointing to a single fact: love is beautiful.

Every day, I fell more and more in love with Brian. We had similar likes and dislikes and although we met online, our bond grew beyond the normal goosebumps and "butterflies in the tummy" kind of love. Nothing beats a man who looks through my tiredness and cares for me, enough to take the world's issues and problems off my plate.

The Wedding Of The Year

The 31st of December, 2019. Our wedding day was magical, inspiring, and nothing short of beautiful. My eyes popped open at 4AM. I could feel my stomach churn with excitement. Today was the day. It was the day I officially became Mrs. Brian. Sure, we were already a well-oiled machine. But there was something about making it official that gave it that permanence along with the announcement to the whole world that we were now one. My mind started to think about the beautiful future that lay ahead of us. I was so convinced that our golden years were going to be the best. I couldn't wait to sit on the porch together holding hands and regaling stories of times past and how beautiful our journey had been. Yes, I could see it now. The thought was so beautiful.

I didn't even realize I was smiling until Christine walked into my room.

"Up already and excited I see." She was also excited. She went to draw the curtains and turned to me. "Gooood morning sunshine! It's a good day to be getting married. Let's get married!" We both giggled with excitement. "I was actually hoping to find you still sleeping. That was your wake up call. But, ah well. "

"It's perfect." I was so happy to have Christine here right now. She was my support system, my great friend.

"Why don't you go shower while I get you some breakfast. The beauty team will soon be here."

"Sounds like a plan," I responded.

We had decided to spend the night before the wedding at the hotel where we were having the wedding. We had booked separate rooms, but we had enjoyed a beautiful dinner together last night, where we both expressed our hopes for the future.

I took my time in the shower, enjoying the warm, luxurious spray of the water on my body. Christine soon knocked on the bathroom door.

"Breakfast is here, hun."

I finished showering and put on the ridiculously soft hotel toweling robe. As we were eating breakfast, a knock came at my door.

"I'll get it," Christine volunteered.

Gaby and Gina walked in looking beautiful and excited.

"Mom!" Boy, was I glad to see these two.

The room soon became busy as the makeup team arrived and started working on the bridal team. The day was well and truly in full swing. Wedding, coming right up!

***

I was ready. The beautiful blushing bride. My friends and daughters snapped their own pictures as I stood there in my gorgeous wedding dress, in full makeup. I was certain Brian would have bought the dress himself if he could. He had been so hands-on during the wedding planning and preps. As I stood looking at myself in the full-length mirror, I smiled. I really was a beautiful bride, ready to be joined to her groom.

"Let's do this," I said as we were cued that it was time. It was definitely shaping up to be a great day.

***

It was his idea to do a skit in the beginning as he was known to be a *playa* (in the words of his friends/family). He had been consistent in his dating of multiple women until we met. At that time, he said he was getting old at 55 and needed to settle down with only one. I, Paula, was the chosen one.

I believed him and never had any reason to doubt it. His actions were very consistent. No secret phone calls, I always knew where he was, and he always answered the phone or texted me if he was busy.

Wedding Vows, Wedding Vibes

When they say *"Nothing lasts forever,"* I didn't expect this axiom to apply to my marriage. That's because two years after we were married, Brian died, and you would think what a blow, but an even bigger blow came after his death. Let me not get ahead of myself. Two years after the wedding, I sat in my living room, watching our wedding video. When Brian had died, nothing had prepared me for what I came to discover. I held the remote control in my hand, like a spy about to watch a surveillance video. With a deep frown, I pressed the play button to the wedding video, hoping to find something I had missed when it all started. Something to help me make sense of everything...something to renew my hope. Or perhaps, something to help me confirm all I had recently discovered about my man.

The groomsmen, dressed in black and white suits with complimenting green ties, were smiling and encouraging my groom. The groom outdid himself, tall and well-built, adorned in his well-fitting black and white suit with a tie to match. I felt like he could calm the fiercest storm when looking at him. He looked like he was about to take on the world by possessing his rarest gift - his bride.

I was a vision in white as I walked majestically into the beautifully arranged ballroom. There I was, tall and fair with shimmery skin, draped in a white flowing gown with a complimenting veil, and accompanied by my beautiful bridesmaids. While some were dressed in blue, others were in teal-colored satin; yet each of them had a radiant smile. I smiled as I saw my daughters looking beautiful in their blue dresses, all excited for me. Priceless. The effort that had gone into making this event memorable was so palpable. The blend of green and white - symbolizing purity and freshness - was perfect, as I was escorted into the grand ballroom to the waiting gaze of my beloved. I looked radiant and gorgeous in my sleeveless bridal gown, my hand guided by my escort, as I walked down the aisle towards my lover.

The theme was love, togetherness, and family. Segregation or separation was not encouraged by any discriminatory seating arrangement; it was an all-inclusive event to promote not just our union, but our families and friends too. We had agreed on this.

And because family meant a great deal to us, we paid homage to our dead too, wishing heaven was only a stone's throw away so they could attend this grand occasion in style. We, however, took solace in the fact that our loved ones were smiling over us, even now, as their pictures decorated the warm ballroom.

Judging by the perfection of this moment, nothing seemed incapable of going wrong. The scene where the groom had worn the "Playa 36" jersey was intended to be a funny act, along with the collection of keys by the best man. Watching this now seemed to send some signals, and I thought to myself: could this have meant more? Was this a red flag that glared at me, and I hadn't recognized it because of the magnificence of the day?

As Brian said his vows, he had everyone's rapt attention, especially mine:

"When I first saw you...
I said 'Oh My,'
I said 'Oh My'
That's my dream...
I needed to dream when it seemed as though I was not going to find anyone to spend my life with...
And then I found it in you, and I've had the most beautiful dream that any man could ever have...
So with these vows Paula, I take you to be my team partner for life
Today, I give you my hand and my heart
I join my life to you, to yours.
From this day forward Paula, you will never be alone, welcome to Team Kryptonite!"

Hitting the nail on the head with sparse but weighty words, he laid bare his soul not only to me but to the teary-eyed audience and well-wishers. He had just committed his life to me, the implication of which had not escaped me. It felt more than a call to duty, I was so engrossed in this moment that I was completely oblivious to the chuckles that came from the audience. I was only focused on him, his words, expressions, and actions. Soaking it all in.

This was a lifelong commitment and to me, every single detail mattered. Everything meant something to me. He had waited for a long time and had chosen me for this lifetime commitment.

As I re-watched this moment, I wondered why his words now rang shallow and hollow. Was it the benefit of hindsight? Did he really put in effort into his vow speech or was it just a script borne out of effort-less blandness? In comparison, my vows had come from a place of deep reflection and dedication.

I had not felt differently about his vows on that day, but now...

Now, it was my turn to say the vows that had been etched deep in my soul.

I saw the abundance of love I had and had felt well up in my eyes as I spoke:

"I was done with dating and had decided that I will be alone forever and then you came into my life like a tornado. My life, as I knew it, was disrupted by a unicorn, a man with no children or ex-wife to contend with. Of course, I gave you the side eye during our first conversations because who, at fifty-something, is still single?"

"But after spending countless hours on the phone and around you, I knew you were special. Not only are you smart, extremely competitive, and handsome, but as I have told my friends, our first conversations left me really curious about you."

"Still cautious, I entrusted my parking lot spies to stay and watch outside the winery while we were on our first date. You've been my ride or die, my community service projects, my fundraising, my volunteer and other extraordinary activities, you've been a check writer, and a DJ for our activities..."

As I re-watched, I saw my groom shift uneasily. I couldn't help but wonder if he had been impatient or irritated as I read my vows. I wasn't sure, so I paused and zoomed in on him to see if I could figure this out. Perhaps it was a figment of my imagination.

I could barely look at the scene where I'd declared him officially mine, promising him a sweet life, companionship, affection, growth, encouragement, patience, understanding, love, and compassion. No doubt, I had kept my own end of the bargain. Had he done the same?

I had not been reckless in choosing a man to love. While dating him, my friends had literally been my spies, ensuring everything he said and did was consistent. God knows I had taken my time – especially since he was in his 50s without an ex-wife or a child.

Not one to be naïve, I ensured all pages were turned and that there were no hidden skeletons anywhere because trust in one's partner is the crucial thread that holds everything together. No skeletons were found, and so I was sure I had found the one based on all he had laid open to me. Embarking on this journey with him felt like the right thing to do because there was no deception. We were both old enough and sure of our decisions. No games and no cutting corners...or so it seemed!

Apparently, it takes more than compatibility to make a union work.

I had ended my vows, and now, I was holding the gaze of the man I had fallen hopelessly in love with. Then, we were joined in holy matrimony.

I did not stop the tears that freely flowed down my cheeks to my chin now even though I had stifled it all through my vows and had sniffed intermittently to get a grip on my emotions, just to stay cool. I tried really hard, albeit unsuccessfully, to still my tears as I finished saying my vows and committed my life to the man I was so sure *I knew.*

We exchanged rings and kissed. We were both happy and ready for this chosen journey even as we stared into each other's eyes. The wedding registrar pronounced:

"...And the life that Brian and Paula used to have, they don't have it anymore, they now have this..."

While holding hands, with my bouquet held like an about-to-be-released trophy, we gleefully jumped the broom according to tradition. It almost felt like our hearts had intertwined into perfect harmony.

We shared our first dance as husband and wife to a romantic ballad playing in the background. We rocked in unison to the song of love in our hearts, and we danced to love. We danced and danced with passion, chatting away like the Prom King and Queen, almost oblivious to everyone else. The world seemed too pale in comparison to the joy of that moment. He gingerly placed his hands on my waist as we swayed, my hands on his solid shoulders and my focus solely on him and for him. It felt like a fairy tale as I bathed in the tenderness of his touch and giggled to his whispers. The video did not capture his whispered words. What was it that he had shared that erupted such wholesome laughter from within me? Was there *any atom* of truth in those words, I now wondered?

As the reception went underway, I briefly took in the scene.

Oh! My heart was bursting with pride. It was such an occasion filled with love, dedication, and good wishes, and the energy radiated through the room. Next, we cut the beautiful wedding cake that was simple, yet so elegantly designed, with colors that matched the occasion's theme. *Velvety white, green, and black.*

We fed each other the cake and laughed, mesmerized by the strange and loving newness that gripped us. People took pictures and gave us their wishes of love and appreciation.

Amidst giggles, I threw my bouquet to the awaiting ladies, and the hall erupted in applause- disbelief etched on the face of the lucky lady who now owned the bouquet. While wearing our team Kryptonite ball caps, we danced once again, joined by the alluring guests who had come to celebrate our love.

No one could deny this fact: it was a beautiful wedding. It was a well-planned event that was meant to have a lasting effect on the memories of everyone witnessing the bond and the marriage itself. As the light faded over this thick-walled ballroom, I again relived the grand moment. I paused to inspect the guests' faces. Perhaps I would catch a glimpse of betraying expressions, hidden secrets that I was not privy to. Yet, all I saw was sincerity and genuine delight. It was too perfect a wedding, so flawless that nothing betrayed the shocking revelation that was to come afterwards.

4

SECTION TWO ~ The Pandemic

A World In Crisis

"Deep breath Paula, deep breath," I told myself as I wiped a tear rolling down my cheek.

I looked up into the mirror as I sat on my dresser. That deep breath finally came, more of a sigh, really. It was like reliving all of it over again. The memory was so crystal clear in my mind as if no time had passed between then and now. I could see it all now as my mind drifted to days gone by...

A World In Crisis

"Have you heard? There's this illness that's taking people in Asia. Apparently, it's airborne so it's pretty contagious. I really feel for the affected people. No one should have to go through that. I heard it on the news this morning when Derek and I were on our way to work." Brian had called me at mid-morning like he usually did.

He really liked listening to the news and knowing what was going on around us. He always had a news tidbit to share with me, so on this particular occasion, I didn't really think much of it; just another bit of news.

We were still in our honeymoon bubble after the wedding when news of the pandemic started to become concerning. It was spreading like a wildfire. Never in a million years did we think it was going to be a literal global pandemic that brought the entire planet to a screeching halt. We were convinced it was one of those sad stories you hear about on the news and then that's it. We had no way of knowing that it was going to show up right in our backyard.

February 2020. The whole world was in a panic. People started going crazy, hoarding. I mean, toilet paper was flying off the shelves like there was no tomorrow. At that point, I thought, "Really, toilet paper?" But I guess we do weird things when we are panicking. It's just what we do as humans. At this point, we knew it wasn't just someone else's problem. It was our problem, collectively. We were all in this together. By March 2020, it was abundantly clear that this was no cold that would quickly pass. Every country in the world was now reporting casualties. Governments all over realized that it was not going to stop, and everyone was grounded. Travel was now at an absolute standstill. It was a full-blown pandemic. Then came the lockdown; nobody could go anywhere. Stay indoors, and wear a mask if you need to get out of the house and only leave for extremely important reasons, like going to the hospital. Brian and I were still pretty much newlyweds, which put things to a halt for us because we had been talking about going away on vacation somewhere special. We hadn't gone away for our honeymoon because when we got married, news of the pandemic was already making the rounds, so as a precaution, we decided to wait it out. But now that everything was shut down, we had to stay at home and wait. If I was being honest, I thought we'd be grounded at home for a couple of weeks tops, but that was not to be the case. It got so bad, and every single person was affected by it. Each time we watched the news, it was heartbreaking. Lives being lost and people getting sick all around. We were in unfamiliar territory. The world as we knew it was in crisis.

The Grapevine

The pandemic had hit us hard, and everyone was struggling to deal with the new normal. Brian and I were no exception. We felt it in every possible way. Shortly after the pandemic started, Brian found out that his good friend, Shaun, had been diagnosed with cancer, had beaten it, and the cancer had come back again. Unfortunately for Brian, he found out about it through the people he carpooled with, and they were not forthright in telling him just how sick Shaun was. Brian was hurt; I could tell. He didn't immediately say it, but I knew. I could tell from his body language and the melancholy look in his eyes. As much as I wanted to tell him not to worry too much about it, I knew in my heart of hearts that nothing was okay about the whole thing. Quite frankly, I was a little upset for him. How could Shaun have kept something like that from him, and then for Brian to find out through the grapevine? It just didn't sit right. The whole thing reeked.

Love thy neighbor

Shaun had always loved my cooking. He was one of those people we enjoyed inviting to dinner because he wholeheartedly enjoyed whatever I put in front of him. A particularly fond memory was when on one occasion, we'd invited Shaun to dinner. He had responded promptly that he'd be coming. Good. I could show off a little and make my famous banana pudding. The first time I'd made it for Brian, he was blown away, so I was pretty sure Shaun would love it too. When it got around to dinner, Shaun had licked his plate clean, much to our amusement. Brian had even joked that Shaun might as well move in with us as a permanent house guest because he really enjoyed my food and was very generous with the compliments. I served the banana pudding, and

I've never seen a whole grown man get up to dance a jig in the middle of a meal. Anyone watching from outside would think he had gotten the biggest news of his life.

"Brian, man, I knew this one was a keeper from day one! Man, your wife has mad kitchen skills. Paula, we need to sign you up for MasterChef." Brian and I couldn't hold in our laughter. The whole time Shaun was talking, he would take a spoonful and do a slow twirl, showing just how much he was enjoying the pudding. Brian turned to me and gave me a peck on the cheek.

In response to Shaun's comment about me being a keeper, he said, "Oh yes, she is. She's quite something, alright."

I felt really good about being Brian's wife with mad culinary skills. I was happy that I made him proud. With that fond memory in my mind, I decided to call Shaun and find out if he would like some of that banana pudding he loved so much since I was also making it for a friend.

"You don't have to ask me twice," he giggled over the phone. He sounded a little raspy, but his voice got that way sometimes, I thought nothing of it.

The pandemic was at its peak, and we had been under lockdown for a month and a half now, though it felt more like ten years! Who knew that being home all the time could be so exhausting!

"Alright then. I'll leave some on the porch, and you can swing by to get it later this evening."

"Thanks, Paula. I'll do that ."

When he came to collect the pudding, I didn't see him, because he just picked it up from where I had left it on the porch and he left. I had no way of knowing how he was doing. In retrospect, I did feel a twinge of guilt pulling at me. Maybe I should have asked him to ring the doorbell and we could have said hi through the window. Maybe I could have picked up on the fact that he wasn't doing alright. Why didn't I think of that before? Ah! This pandemic messed a lot of things up.

The Cat Is Out Of The Bag

A few months went by, and Brian found out from his coworker, Derek that Shaun was sick. Brian was taken aback by the news. Shaun had been sick for all these months and had said nothing? He chose not to believe it off the cuff.

"Well, if that were true, I'm sure we would have known about it, right?" Brian was adamant that Shaun could never get sick and not say anything, " I guess this lockdown is making people lose it, talking all crazy and stuff."

But deep down, Brian knew that it was true. What he couldn't decide was why Shaun had kept it such a secret, well, at least from him. With all these questions swimming around in his head, Brian decided to rally up the guys so they could all go over to Shaun's house to hang out with him, never mind the lockdown rules. His friend was sick, and he was going to be there for him. One of the many qualities I loved about my husband. He truly cared about those he loved. You could trust that he would be there in your darkest hour. He was the type of guy who was a pillar of strength to his nearest and dearest. It made me all happy inside just to know he was someone that could be counted on.

He called Derek early one morning, but it went straight to voicemail, so he left a message for him: "Hey, man. What do you say we all head on over to Shaun's to see how he's doing, seeing that he's sick and all? Call me." He didn't call back. Brian called him a second time and Derek told him he'd let him know once he'd been in touch with Shaun to ask when they could come over. A week passed and Derek hadn't said anything, so Brian called again for the third time.

"Sorry, man, I didn't really get around to calling Shaun. Maybe we should wait it out a bit, you know, with the lockdown and all."

Brian confided in me shortly afterwards.

"Hey hun, is it just me, or is Derek being cagey about the whole thing with Shaun? I mean, the guy is sick and I think it would be great if we saw him as a show of solidarity. But I guess with the whole pandemic in full swing, it would be better to wait it out. Let's see."

Seven months went by, and Brian found out that Shaun was even sicker than he thought. He came home upset, and that night got a phone call letting him know that Shaun had passed away. This had us both reeling. It was hard to believe that someone we were once close to had died, and we didn't even know he was sick! It just made it that much harder to process.

"I knew it! I knew I should have gone to see him when I had the chance," he sobbed in my lap. It was hard to watch. He had clearly cared deeply about Shaun. It shouldn't have happened the way it had. All the secrecy around Shaun's illness, and his being in the hospital the whole time before he died. I really couldn't comprehend what was happening. Something was definitely up.

5

The Dark Cloud

The Dark Cloud

When Brian found out that Shaun had died, he was even more upset because he felt like his friend Derek and others had not been honest with him about Shaun's health. He was not given an opportunity to see him or get closure. Brian stopped talking to Derek and the other people who knew about Shaun's ill health. It was like watching someone else die because it changed Brian somehow. He became more somber. A dark cloud seemed to constantly hang over him ever since Shaun's death. He would get in the same car as Derek and the others, go to work, and come back together, but Brian didn't talk to them because of his anger. He was livid. How they managed to be in the same space without killing each other is a miracle in itself. I wondered why there had been so much secrecy around Shaun's illness and subsequent death. Did something happen that I wasn't aware of? Was there bad blood? These questions kept simmering in my mind. I couldn't ask Brian because he was pretty shaken and upset; it wouldn't have been a good idea.

I was afraid Shaun's passing would put a significant strain on our marriage, but to my delight, Brian still remained the caring, devoted husband, albeit with a chip on his shoulder. I got it. I would be upset, too, under the circumstances. But when he was home with me, he was still my prince charming and made sure I knew that I was loved, and I felt it. I did all I could to make him feel supported. I cooked all his favorite meals back-to-back and stood by him when he was melancholic. *For better, for worse. For richer, for poorer. In sickness or in health.* I was his ride-or-die.

Secrets And Lies

After Brian passed, I discovered the real reason that Derek did not tell Brian about Shaun's health condition was because of two things. First, when Brian had been dating a girl named Charlene, before I met him, he broke up with her because when she got cancer, Brian pulled a gun to her head, and basically told her, "If you don't get the fuck out of my house, I'm going to kill you." Scared and hurt, she had packed her things and went to Shaun's house because she had nowhere else to go. Shaun was upset with Brian, but he never said anything to him. Brian had mercilessly left Charlene in the lurch, in terms of taking up for her or being supportive.

When I heard about this, I was completely shocked. I never saw that one coming. I honestly couldn't see Brian doing something like that. The man couldn't harm a fly! Who was this Brian I was hearing about? Not mine. I've got to be honest, it was hard to hear and a bitter pill to swallow. The fact that he had pulled a gun on his sick, then-girlfriend made me sick to my stomach. Now I understood why Shaun had kept his cancer diagnosis hush-hush. He clearly hadn't forgiven Brian for not supporting Charlene in her time of need, and now that he also had cancer, he hadn't trusted Brian to handle it well.

Unfortunately, I was never able to speak with Brian about this as I found this out a month after he died. I guess it was a shock for me; hearing this from Shaun's mother and then from Charlene herself. All I could think was that, *No one deserves to be treated in that way.* Sure, he had mentioned that he had a long-time girlfriend called Charlene, but he never once told me that he had treated her so poorly. Clearly no remorse there. I was appalled.

As I sat there listening to Shaun's mom and Charlene's explanation, I couldn't help but feel a sense of betrayal. I had thought I knew him so well, but it turned out that there was a whole other side to him that I had never even imagined. It was as if a veil had been lifted, and I was seeing him for the very first time. I had been living with a stranger, he was no longer my husband. He was an imposter.

I couldn't imagine how Charlene must have felt when Brian pointed that gun at her. It was a cruel and heartless thing to do, and I was horrified that someone I cared about could be capable of something so monstrous. But at the same time, I couldn't help but feel sorry for Brian too. What made him do such a horrific thing.

Over the next few days, I struggled to reconcile my feelings about the whole thing, and about my now deceased husband. On the one hand, I was angry and disappointed in him. On the other hand, I wondered what else had been hidden from me. I knew that everyone has flaws and makes mistakes and that forgiving someone is often the best thing you can do for yourself. But I also knew that the memories I had of us would never be the same again. I felt it deep within me. And just like that, the thoughts and memories of a happy marriage disintegrated right before my eyes. The man I thought I knew had turned out to be someone completely different, and I wasn't sure if I was ready to accept that. But with time, I began to see that there was a lot more to him that was hidden. I was constantly reminded of why I had said yes to this man in the first place. He had my heart. For the sake of my sanity, I prayed, truly prayed, that there would be no more surprises up the road. Looking back, maybe I should have prayed for strength instead, because the road was about to get bumpier! This revelation was more than I could handle. I should have known that this revelation was a crack in the facade. The man I thought I knew simply didn't exist.

BROKEN PIECES

Perhaps my mind had conjured him up and kept him there for as long as I fed the fantasy. In hindsight, this was the other shoe dropping, but it didn't compute at the time. I got to get a glimpse of the real Brian, the unabridged version.

A Man's Man

Shaun's stubbornness was always a defining trait of his personality. He had always been fiercely independent, and he never wanted anyone's help, even when he was clearly struggling. It was this same pride that made him refuse to let anyone see him in his weakened state when he got sick. He was too proud to be seen as weak or vulnerable, and he thought that people would pity him if they saw him in his condition. This was a source of frustration for his friends, especially Brian. Brian was used to being there for his friends, and he felt like he had been shut out by Shaun. He didn't understand why Shaun hadn't wanted him to see him, and he felt like he had been deliberately kept in the dark. This feeling of being shut out only made things worse for Brian, and he withdrew from the people who knew about Shaun's condition. If anyone mentioned them, his comment was always, "Fuck that person, fuck this person. They kept Shaun from me."

It wasn't that Brian didn't care about the other guys, it was just that he didn't know how to deal with his own emotions. Grief was a foreign concept to him and he didn't know how to process it. He was used to being the strong one, the one who took care of others, and he didn't know how to handle the fact that he couldn't help Shaun and now he was gone. But even though Shaun didn't want anyone to see him in his weakened state, he still wanted his friends to know what was going on. He knew they would worry about him, so he had confided in Derek about his condition. For Brian, this only added salt to the wound because as far as he was concerned, he was closer to Shaun than Derek was, so he had found it difficult to understand why Shaun hadn't told him too. No one also ever told Brian that Shaun knew everything that had happened with Charlene. It was something of an open secret. Shaun and the guys knew, but Brian didn't know they knew. They didn't want to hurt him or make him feel some type of way.

Well, he eventually got to the truth. Derek later opened up to him and told him Shaun and the guys had known about the whole situation with Charlene. Brian was dumbfounded. So, all this time everyone knew what had happened and no one said anything. Perhaps he could have gotten a chance to fix things with Shaun if he knew that something was wrong. He had no idea Shaun was mad at him for what he had done to Charlene. I can honestly say, hand on heart, that was one of Brian's biggest regrets in life - not being able to set things straight with Shaun before he passed on.

Healing And Forgiveness

The power of love and forgiveness is genuinely remarkable. It can heal even the deepest of wounds and bring people together in ways that one never thought possible. After learning about what happened with Brian and Charlene, I was convinced I could never forgive my late husband for what he had done. But I realized that I had to somehow let it go for my own sanity and peace of mind. Forgiveness is one thing, but choosing to let go so something won't haunt you, is quite another.

The pandemic period was tough on everyone, and it forced us to confront some difficult truths about ourselves and the world around us. But it has also shown us the power of love and forgiveness. We have seen communities come together to support each other, and we have seen individuals rise up and show compassion in the face of adversity. Even through the mire of Shaun's death and the revelation about how poorly Brian had treated Charlene, I still felt optimistic that everything would turn out fine. I was in for a rude awakening.

BROKEN PIECES

6

SECTION THREE ~ Beginning of The End

You Think You Know Someone

The call came early on a Monday morning. I could hear my phone ring as I stirred from my sleep. Gees! Who would be calling at this hour? With one eye still shut, hoping to retain my sleep while I dealt with this rude awakening (literally!), I reached out for it. See, this is why Brian always told me to turn my phone off when going to bed. No distractions. After today, I was ready to follow that sound advice. I checked the time on my bedside table. 3:00 A.M. This had better be good. I checked to see who was calling, but I didn't recognize the number. I was tempted to ignore it and go back to sleep but a small part of me was curious to find out who had the gall to be calling me at 3 o'clock in the morning.

"Good morning ma'am. I'm calling you from Sunninghill Medical Center...." My heart went into a tizz. A call from the hospital at odd hours was never good news. I tried to brace myself.

"You were listed as Brian's emergency contact that's why we're calling you. I'm calling to inform you that your husband has been involved in a car accident. He was brought in, in an ambulance and rushed straight into surgery because he's lost a lot of blood..." Was she about to tell me that my man was dead?! I started to shake.

BROKEN PIECES

"How is he?' I asked shakily.

"As far as I can tell, he just came out of surgery. It would be great if you could come in and talk to his doctor."

"Yes, of course. I'll be there as soon as I can."

She went on to give me his room number so I could head straight there when I came in. When the call ended, I was partly relieved that he was still alive, and still shaken by the news that he had been involved in an accident. I got out of bed and started pacing around our bedroom trying to calm the adrenaline that was coursing through me. I could hardly think, so I went downstairs to get some water. As I got to the landing, I couldn't help but notice how it was so still, so quiet, like nothing had happened. Tragedy had a way of sneaking up on you and striking at the peak of your peace, and just like that, it was done; like it never happened. Like a storm, it came and destroyed stuff then as quickly as it came, it's gone again. I turned on the lights in the living room and kitchen. I decided to stay down here for a bit to clear my head. After a tall glass of water, some of that brain fog started to dissipate. My mind started to work.

Wait, the lady said she was calling from Sunninghill Medical Center. That was right here, less than a 15-minute drive from our home. Brian had left on Friday for a business meeting in Texas. He was meant to get back today, Monday. I wasn't expecting him home until early this evening. What was he doing back home before then? And why hadn't he called me to tell me he was back? Perhaps he had wanted to surprise me. He liked doing that a lot. But something shifted in me uncomfortably. I quickly pushed it aside and put it down to the emotions I was feeling. Then it hit me again. Brian was lying in the hospital unconscious, fighting for his life, and here I was, his wife, thinking about why he didn't call to tell me he had come back home early. A wave of guilt surged through me. I got up from the kitchen chair and went back upstairs. I wasn't sure what I should bring for him. I should have asked if they'd gotten his belongings. But just in case, I decided to pack an overnight bag for him with the essentials. He would be grateful when he regained consciousness. I found myself fussing about what to take, it took me a good hour to pack a basic overnight. I then got ready as I saw the time approaching 6 o'clock. By 6 AM, I was at the hospital reception signing in. I headed straight for his room.

He was awake when I got there. He looked so fragile and vulnerable hooked up to a machine, blood bags, and some other IV fluid. A far cry from the man I knew. I walked up to him and planted a gentle kiss on his lips.

"Baby, you had me worried. An accident...awww, my poor baby."

He managed to put his hand on my arm.

"No, don't talk, it's alright. Rest for now. You've been through a lot."

It looked like he wanted to talk, but I encouraged him to rest instead. I pulled up a chair next to his bed and held his hand as I watched him drift back to sleep, with a slight smile. I didn't want him to see the worry and concern that I felt inside. That's the last thing he needed. As he slept, the doctor popped his head through the door.

"Ah! The wife, I presume? I'm Doctor Akinwale," he said as he came into the room.

"Yes. I'm Paula."

He looked at the tablet that was in his hand.

"Yep, it says here you're his emergency contact. Ok, so as you already know, your husband was in a car accident, and he was rushed here by some EMTs who were the first to respond on-site. When he came in, he had lost a lot of blood and was unconscious. The good news is that his injuries did not affect his head or brain, but he did sustain a couple of nasty cuts and bruises and there was some significant swelling. The surgery he underwent was to stop any internal bleeding and we were happy to find that no significant damage was done to any of his internal organs. With that said, we are optimistic that he will make a full recovery, but for now, we want to see the swelling recede before we can one hundred percent say he's out of the woods. Of course, he is going to need lots of rest to facilitate his recovery."

I was taking it all in, and the doctor saw the overwhelm of everything that he was telling me written all over my face.

"Hey, this is good news. Considering the EMT report about the accident, he's been really lucky to make it out alive."

"Thank you Doc." I could feel relief starting to wash over me. Brian was going to be ok.

"Do you have any questions for me?"

"Yeah, and I don't know if you have any answers for this one. What happened? The accident, I mean."

"Well, as far as we know and from what the EMTs have told us, his car was smashed into on the driver's side by another vehicle. I'm not so sure about the details. But you can contact the local PD. Emergency services did log in their report with them, so they may have more answers for you on that front."

"That's really helpful. Again, thanks a lot Dr. Akinwale. I'm glad for all your help."

"Glad we could help. We should have another update on your husband's condition in the next 24 hours."

"Thank you."

I was just so grateful that he made it out on the other side. But how did he get rammed by another vehicle? My next stop was the police station from the hospital. I wanted to find out everything that had happened to my man. I sat with Brian for another half hour as he slept before I told a nurse I was leaving and would be grateful if they could give me a call when he woke up. She agreed to do so, and I left to pay a visit to the cops.

The End

The police report on the accident shed more light on what happened. Apparently, the driver of the other vehicle had tried to beat the red light and hit Brian's car at the intersection. The police suspected the driver didn't think anyone would be on the road at that time of the morning, that's why he tried to beat the light. And no he wasn't drunk. They also informed me that the other driver had sustained injuries as well. My heart went out to the other driver. I hoped he, too, would make a good recovery. As I walked out of the station, I made a mental note to call his family and our friends the moment I got home. I had hardly gotten into my car when my phone rang. It was the same number that had called me early this morning - the hospital. I told myself to remember to save the number to my phone. I figured they were calling me to let me know he was awake.

"This is Paula."

"Hi, Paula. I'm calling you from Sunninghill Medical Center. We need you to come into the hospital."

"Is everything alright?"

"The doctor will talk to you when you're here. I'm not sure what it is about."

Something in me knew that something was wrong. Did he need another surgery? Was there a complication with the first one? With these possibilities running through my mind, I drove back to the hospital and rushed toward Brian's room, but Dr. Akinwale intercepted me on my way there.

"Paula. Thanks for coming back so quickly. Can we sit somewhere?"

"Doc, you're scaring me. What's going on?"

"Let's sit." He gently guided me to a bench that was close by.

"Paula, I'm sorry to have to tell you that Brian did not make it..." I didn't hear the rest. My mind switched off, my ears started ringing and suddenly I could not breathe. I felt faint and the next thing, it was dark.

BROKEN PIECES

When I opened my eyes, I was on a hospital bed hooked up to an IV. Confused, I looked around to see if there were any hospital personnel I could talk to. A nurse was standing on the other side of my bed.

"Hey, what happened?"

"You went into shock. Your blood sugar was up so the IV will help with that. You should be feeling fine in no time at all."

"But, why was I in shock?"

Then, like a forceful wave, it came crashing down and hit me again. Brian was gone. I couldn't help the cry that escaped my lips. It was that of pain. No one ever prepares you for something like this. When Brian and I got married, I thought we had our whole lives ahead of us. We were going to sit on the porch, holding hands and looking back on the beautiful life we'd built together. Now, barely two years after we got married, he was gone. I could feel the pain crush into me relentlessly, wave after wave. It felt like my heart had been ripped out of my chest, the very breath squeezed out of my lungs. I was crying openly and sobbing uncontrollably. A woman I didn't see came in, took me in her arms, and allowed me to cry. She didn't say anything; she just held me. When I came up for air, the woman let me out of her embrace and sat in the chair by my bed. She introduced herself as the grief counselor at the hospital. She talked to me about what had just happened, and I, in between sobs, told her I couldn't believe Brian was gone. She was really compassionate, and I was glad she was there with me then.

"Well, Paula, I took the liberty of calling the second person on your emergency contact list, Christine. She is on her way as we speak."

"Thank you," I managed shakily.

A few minutes later, Christine walked in and rushed to the side of my bed.

"Oh, Paula." We held each other and cried for a few minutes. The grief counselor went out discreetly, giving us the necessary space to grieve.

"How did this happen Chris? How could this happen? We just started our lives together and now it's over just like that?"

"I wish I had the answers my darling. It all is so unfair."

Dust to Dust

The funeral was beautiful. Much like our wedding, the turnout and show of support were positively overwhelming. I was grateful to have all our friends and family there with me. The church service was at his family church in Virginia led by his family members. They were engaging yet calm. They spoke with empathy and compassion. It was only natural for me to reach out to them and ask them to conduct the funeral. They didn't hesitate. I was grateful for their support. Brian was laid to rest a few days after he passed at Sunninghill Medical Center.

***

I wouldn't have known who she was if Derek, Brian's friend, hadn't pointed her out to me.

"Hey, Paula. What's Charlene doing here?" Derek asked.

"Charlene? Who's that?"

"You know, Brian's ex."

"Oh yeah. What do you mean she's here?"

"She's right there in the living room with the other guests." He pointed her out.

After the church service guests were invited back to my cousin's house for food and comfort.

How did she even know to come? Curious, I decided to go talk to her.

"Hi...Charlene, is it?"

"Oh, hi. You must be Paula. Listen, I am so sorry for your loss. Brian was a good man."

She genuinely looked distraught that he was gone.

"How did you know about his passing?" I was curious to know what Charlene of all people would be doing here. She looked down at her hands. She was a bit fidgety, and avoided eye contact with me. At that moment Christine arrived.

"Hey, what's going on here? Paula, how are you holding up hun?"

"As good as can be expected under the circumstances."

Christine gave Charlene a once over before turning to me with a questioning look. She must have seen the confusion in my eyes because she pulled both of us aside, away from the people.

"Is everything alright? You both look terribly uncomfortable."

Charlene quickly introduced herself.

"Charlene, as in Brian's ex Charlene?" Christine queried.

Charlene shifted nervously. "Yes."

"What are you doing here?" As I said before, Christine was a straight shooter.

"The morning Brian died, he was coming from my place," Charlene explained.

I nearly dropped the water I was holding. Had Brian been cheating on me this whole time?

Charlene quickly added. "And no, we weren't having an affair. You see, I haven't been doing great and Brian heard about it and came to help me. He said he felt bad about putting me out the way he did, so he offered to help me whenever I needed it."

"What do you mean after putting you out the way he did?" I queried.

And that's when Charlene told me about Brian pulling a gun on her. Christine and I were both shocked. We got confirmation of this a month later from Shaun's mom.

When Charlene told me, part of me was glad he had been trying to do the right thing, but the other part was upset about all the secrecy. I mulled it over in the back of my mind, wondering why Brian would keep something like that a secret. Had he also been lying about the business trip to Texas altogether?

When it was all over, and everyone had gone back home, my girls and Christine stayed with me. They made sure I rested a lot because they didn't want another incident like the one where I collapsed at the hospital. I couldn't say how long these wonderful women in my life were around taking care of me. I lost track of time like it no longer mattered. What mattered was the incessant pain that I felt. The emptiness that was there because my man was gone. But that was about to change. I still kept what Charlene had told me in the back of my mind.

Over the next few weeks, I started getting better and learning to do life without Brian. It was an adjustment, but I was getting there. I decided to get back to my cooking as it always brought me so much joy. I started cooking most of Brian's favorite dishes until I was ready to cook other things. Honestly, it was cathartic.

Ashes to Ashes

It was one of those days when I wanted to make the food Brian liked to eat. I was missing him and decided to make something that reminded me of him. I was busy in the kitchen when the doorbell rang. Probably someone who had come to check in on me. The support and well-wishes were incredible. As I opened the door, I was pleasantly surprised to see Dwayne, our lawyer. Dwayne was someone I knew through the work that I did and he had become a dear friend. I had reached out to him at his office to find out about Brian's will reading, but he hadn't been in so I'd left a message.

"Well, hello! Come on in," I invited him inside.

"I didn't expect that a phone call would turn into a visit," I laughed.

"Well, yes. I was actually meaning to come in and see you anyway but at a more appropriate time. So when you called, it was perfect timing."

"Well, thank you for coming all the way. And, oh, thanks for coming to the funeral. I really appreciated seeing you and Linda there. And thanks again for the beautiful flowers." He and Linda had been married for decades and seeing them always made me feel joyful and optimistic.

"You don't have to thank me, Paula. How are you holding up?"

I sighed, "Well, you know, some days are better than others. But I've found such a release in my cooking so I'm getting there."

"I'm glad to hear that. It's especially great for us folk who enjoy your cooking," he laughed.

"Speaking of cooking, can I offer you a slice of lemon cake? It's freshly baked."

"Oooh, how could I say no to that! Please." He rubbed his hands together in anticipation.

"I'm glad to see you brought your appetite." We both laughed.

I served him a slice of the lemon cake I'd baked earlier, together with some coffee."

"Thanks, Paula," he said as he dug in.

'Hmmm, as good as I remember it."

I smiled. It felt good to have someone appreciate the food I made again. Brian always did that. He was my personal food taster and cheerleader. He really loved my cooking. Dwayne polished the cake slice easily. I offered him another slice but he declined.

"If I keep eating, I won't be able to work."

"Ok then, let's sit over here by the dining room table."

When we were both settled in, Dwayne looked at me grimly. He clearly had something he needed to talk to me about.

"There's no better way to say this, so I'll just rip the bandaid right off."

7

House of Cards

House Of Cards

"You called about Brian's will reading. Well, there is no will."

I was confused. I looked at Dwayne with a frown. " What do you mean? He was always talking about his will; at some point, he even told me he'd updated it."

"Well, if there is a will, he didn't do it with us. If he had, we would have read the will soon after the funeral."

My frown deepened. This made no sense.

"Ok, so you think it's possible that he used another lawyer for his will?" But why would he?

"It's possible. So I also checked to see if his will was lodged elsewhere. It's not. There simply isn't one."

So what did this all mean? Suddenly I felt betrayed all over again. Not so long ago, Shaun's mom had corroborated Charlene's story about how Brian had treated her poorly, now this! Why would Brian lie to me about his will? Was he hiding something?

Dwayne hesitated before speaking again, and I could sense that he was hesitant to deliver the news, "There's more, Paula."

BROKEN PIECES

More! How on earth could there possibly be more?! At that moment, I knew I wasn't going to like what I was going to hear. I couldn't even brace myself.

"When I did the checks about the will, I discovered a whole lot of other stuff. It appears that Brian had not been paying the mortgage or utility bills in almost two years. He also took all the money out of his 401k and had a loan against it."

My heart sank as I heard this news. I had been giving him money towards that, like clockwork. In fact, before we got married, he paid for it. I know because the evidence was there when we filed joint taxes together in the first year reflecting 2019 and 2020. I also gave him money typically on the first day of the month to cover the mortgage. If for some reason I had not sent it by mid-day, he would send me a text as a reminder. So yes I was taken aback to hear that he hadn't paid the mortgage in nearly two years. So where did the money that I had given him go? What had he been up to? It's like Dwayne was talking about some other Brian; a stranger. Not my Brian. My sweet, loving husband, Brian. It certainly didn't sound like the same man. Why would Brian do this? It made no sense. He had just bought a $80,000 used Tesla for crying out loud. The very car that he'd been in an accident with. My head was spinning at this point. I felt weak.

"That's not all," Dwayne said.

Someone kill me now. More?!!!!

"Brian also owed over $200,000 in back taxes..."

As he spoke, I felt like someone was throwing stones at me because boy, did it hurt. It hurt so much. I felt like I was shutting down.

Dwayne continued, "I'm sorry to have to tell you that Brian didn't have any money left when he passed on. He died with only $700 to his name and about $1000 in credit card debt."

I couldn't believe what I was hearing. I had trusted Brian completely, and now it was clear that it had all been one big lie. How on earth did I not know about his financial issues? It was like he had been living a double life, like one of those double agents in the movies.

|71|

JANIS PARKER PRESSLEY

Dwayne paused before continuing, "There is one more thing. It appears that there are several liens on the house. IRS, Home Owners Association, a second mortgage, lawsuit, traffic tickets, and more. I'm afraid that these liens have eaten up the equity that you were planning to use to move to Virginia."

"A lawsuit?"

"Yes, it says here," he looked at his tablet as he spoke. "It says an ex-girlfriend called Charlene filed a lawsuit against him, but he hadn't settled that so there was a lien on the house for that."

Wait! Hold up. Suddenly it all hit me. The only reason Brian was being nice to Charlene was not because he was a good guy. He was trying to get himself out of the sticky pickle with the whole lawsuit. And that's why he had never told me about helping her out. It's because it was all lies. He didn't care about her...or me. Brian only cared about Brian. So not only had he fooled me, he had done the same with Charlene. All the secrets and lies just pointed to how selfish and uncaring he really was. And I hadn't seen any of it.

I felt a lump forming in my throat as I realized the full extent of Brian's deception. He had not only hidden his financial indiscretions from me, but he had also lied about the equity in the house, selling me a future that didn't even exist! It felt like the ground had been pulled out from under me. And the funny thing was that we were making plans to sell the house in a few years and take the equity - about $400,000, and use that to move across the country to Virginia on some land that had been left to him by his great, great grandmother. According to him we could just move there and build a house. In reality, the equity had been eaten up by his liens. No wonder he was constantly monitoring the real estate market and talking about how much equity he had to move! He was fleecing me the whole time.

"So what does this all mean, Dwayne? What happens to all this debt?

Dwayne sighed before he responded. "Well, most likely, all these guys are going to try and collect from you, being that you're his legally surviving spouse."

"Wait, what! Are you telling me right now, in my house, that I inherited debt?! Dwayne, what are you saying to me right now?" I could feel the anger boiling hot within me. The nerve, the gall of this guy. How dare he try to ruin me financially and he was even doing it posthumously! I should have done a prenup like my sister had suggested. She was concerned that I didn't really know this guy from a bar of soap and should protect my assets. Adamantly, I had told her that wasn't love, and certainly not Brian's and mine. We were always open and honest with each other. We trusted each other, we both didn't feel like we needed one. I had taken the time to make sure I knew him before tying the knot so I had been confident that everything was all good. Now I feel naive. How did I not see this? How had this man pulled the wool over my eyes? No kidding, I had lived in his home with a stranger this whole time. A stranger who'd used me and lied to me to get his way. What hurt the most was that it took his death for me to realize who Brian really was.

Dwayne looked at me sympathetically. All the emotions I was feeling were obviously etched on my face. "I'm sorry to have to deliver this news to you, Paula. I know it's a lot to take in."

I nodded silently, unable to speak. The reality of the situation was slowly sinking in, and I knew that it was going to take some time to come to terms with everything that I'd just heard.

"But let's talk more about what we can do when you're up for it. I think this has been a lot for one day."

I just shook my head in disbelief. Never in a million years did I think this would be my life. Now I had to fight for my financial security. A security I'd paid for with my sweat, hard work and determination. And just like that it was being threatened!

"Dwayne, at this point I don't even know what to do. I can't even think straight, it's all so overwhelming."

"That's alright. I completely understand. Why don't I give you a couple of days and we can talk again in about a week or so?"

"Yeah, ok. Thanks, Dwayne. I appreciate it."

I saw Dwayne off to the front door and as soon as I closed the door behind him, the floodgates opened up. I cried and cried and cried until I couldn't find any more tears. *Damn you Brian! How could you?* This somehow felt worse than the day they told me he hadn't made it, at the hospital. At least then, I was mourning someone I knew and loved deeply. But now I wasn't even sure who this person was that I had just given over two years of my life to. The shock of finding out how much of a sham this all was came hurtling down like a house of cards.

A Domino Effect

I sat on the floor of the entrance, my back to the front door. I was too stunned to even think or do anything. I just sat there crying for hours, I had no strength left in me. I was no longer mourning my late sweet husband. I was mourning the couple I thought we were, the love that was so obviously one-sided; because if he really loved me, he wouldn't have done this to me. Love is kind. Yes, and Brian had been anything but. Then the self-blame started. How could I not have seen this? Was I so desperate for him to love me that I subconsciously shut it all down? I mean, I wasn't even actively looking for love when Brian waltzed into my life via Hinge. As I said previously, I was good. But he came along and became the person that I could not live without. He became my everything, my Mr. Perfect. But of course, I knew now that was far from the truth. Instead, he had used me and lied to me without even batting an eyelid.

I spent the next few days trying to make sense of it all. I even stopped cooking again. Christine and my daughters had just gone back to their places so I was all alone. I guess I needed to be alone to process everything, process the fact that I had loved a con artist.

It was hard to come to terms with the fact that I had been so blind to Brian's true nature. But as the days went by, I realized that it wasn't my fault. Brian had been a master at his craft - deception. He had fooled many people besides me. Charlene was one of those people. How else could he have kept up his financial indiscretions? I knew that I had to face the reality of the situation and start figuring out how to move forward.

***

I called Dwayne to discuss the liens on the house and what could be done about them. It wasn't going to be easy, but I was determined to fight for what was rightfully mine. We agreed to meet at his office in two days' time.

As I sat in the small conference room of Dwayne's legal offices, I was nervous, but determined to find a solution to the problem of the liens on the house and Brian's debts.

Dwayne walked in with an associate and paralegal. "Paula, thank you for coming in today. This is Leah, my associate, and that's Ted, our paralegal. Ted will be taking notes of what we'll discuss, which will be later drafted into a legal document and a copy sent to you as well. Leah is here because she's going to help me on this case."

I nodded in acknowledgment as he introduced me to his team.

"As you know, there are several liens on your property, and we need to discuss a plan for addressing them."

I nodded, "Yes, I understand. I just want to make sure that I'm not held liable for Brian's actions. I had no idea that his financial affairs were this bad, and I don't want to be punished for something that I didn't even know about to begin with."

Dwayne chimed in, "That's exactly why we're here, Paula. Leah and I have been discussing your case, and we believe that we have a plan that can help you get out from under the liens and any liability for Brian's debts."

I leaned forward, "I'm all ears. What's the plan?"

Leah took a deep breath, "Well, it's not going to be easy, but we believe that we can challenge the liens in court. We've done some research, and we think that there are some legal loopholes that we can use to our advantage."

"What kind of loopholes?"

Leah continued, "Well, for one thing, some of the liens are not properly documented. There are also some errors in the paperwork that was filed. We believe that we can use these discrepancies to argue that the liens are invalid. So, you can't be held liable for Brian's debts unless you co-signed on any of his loans or credit cards. As far as we can tell, you had no involvement in his financial affairs, and therefore you have no responsibility for his debts."

Dwayne added, "And even if we can't get all the liens dismissed, we can argue deniability. We can prove that you had no prior knowledge of Brian's financial indiscretions because you consistently gave him the money to pay for the mortgage, which he never did. We will need your financial statements, of course, and all the receipts you have to prove this. We will also show that you've always paid your bills and mortgage on time before Brian came along. What I'm saying, Paula, is that we need to show the court that Brian deliberately deceived you. If we can successfully establish you as the victim in all this, we can get you exonerated from all this debt. The goal is to minimize the impact on your finances and credit score."

I breathed a sigh of relief, "That's good to hear. So what's the next step?"

Leah responded, "The next step is to file the necessary paperwork to challenge the liens. It's going to take some time and effort, but we believe that we can get a positive outcome for you."

Dwayne nodded, "And we'll be with you every step of the way. We're committed to helping you get through this and move on with your life."

I felt a sense of gratitude towards Dwayne and Leah. I knew that the road ahead would be difficult, but with their help, I felt more confident that I could overcome the challenges and start fresh.

"Thank you both for your help. I really appreciate it."

Dwayne smiled, "It's our pleasure, Paula. We'll do everything we can to make this process as smooth as possible for you."

***

BROKEN PIECES

I also reached out to a therapist to help me process the emotions that I was feeling. It wasn't easy to admit that I needed help, but I knew that it was the right thing to do. Slowly but surely, I started to put the pieces of my life back together. It was a long and difficult process, but I knew that I was strong enough to get through it. Eventually, I had to open up to Christine and my daughters about everything that had happened. I invited all three of them for dinner on a Friday night. I didn't immediately let on that something was wrong. It was only after dinner that I told them everything that had happened.

"Floored! I'm just floored. I cannot believe that Brian was this whole other person. How did he even fool all of us?" Christine was shocked.

"Oh, Mom. You didn't deserve this," Gaby and Gina enveloped me in a hug. They were both crying.

"We are so sorry. So,so sorry."

At this point, we were all in tears. My daughters, for the pain they could see in my eyes, and Christine, for what I'd been through. It was difficult telling them about it all, but they were very supportive.

***

It could have been the fact that I had lost my husband and not so long after, found out that he was a stranger. Or maybe it was because I was just in pain over everything. It could have been that I was at a place where I was exhausted by the whole ordeal. Whatever it was, a few months later, I lost my job. I was traumatized. Thank goodness for my therapist who had been helping me through it all, giving me helpful coping mechanisms. I was even more glad that I had the support of Gina, Gaby, and Christine. The day they let me go, I didn't cry; I wasn't too upset. Had I now gotten accustomed to bad news and pain? It felt like one other thing that happened that I had to deal with. Between paying my legal bills to ensure I wasn't embroiled in Brian's financial mess and trying to make sure the bills and mortgage to my house were up to date, I was paying out quite a significant amount of money. Losing my job at such a time was like the last card falling from my

| 77 |

house of cards. It was like a domino effect. One tile falls, and they all go tumbling down.

New Beginnings

I had to move in with Christine, mostly because I had gone through so much and being alone was the last thing I needed. Also, it gave me time to breathe. I needed to be away from that house. The house I had shared with a stranger. It suddenly felt eerie and it hardly felt like home. I had let that man into my life, my house, and my heart. And look where that left me. Once all the legal trouble was done, I was planning to sell the house and move away from the general vicinity. It felt like a crime scene that I didn't want any part of. I just wanted a fresh start. I needed to just be. My therapist also thought it was a great idea, but she advised me to start small - visit a friend for the weekend, go away for a few days, gradually move from the house, and then make the final commitment of letting it go. She said it was a healing process and any sudden moves could cause more harm than good.

So, while losing my job was hard, it wasn't the end of the world after the experiences I'd had. In fact, I had always wanted to go out on my own, but I didn't want to do anything that would jeopardize my daughters' futures so I put my head down and worked. We had a good roof over our heads, delicious food on our table, and decent clothes on our backs. I couldn't risk throwing all that away if it didn't work out. I was a single mom and needed to do everything in my power to make sure we were well taken care of. It had been 20 years and I'd worked hard and gotten to a good place in my career. I was good at what I did. Even now as I sat in Christine's living room while she was out at work, I thought about the possibilities of going out on my own. Perhaps it took my safety net being taken from under me to get me going. I went up to my room and pulled out my journal where I had jotted down the ideas and dreams that I had for my own business. All things work together. When a door closes, a window opens up. For the first time in a long time, I felt like the air was light and crisp. For so long it had felt suffocating and unbreathable. That's because my life lay in shambles before me. But today, I saw it from a different perspective and it took my life being blown to smithereens, I looked at the broken pieces and thought, *Imagine the beautiful mosaic I can make with these.* Because the truth is, broken crayons still color. I was not just broken by my experience. I was beautifully broken. Out of the brokenness came a beauty that I didn't even know was there. Even after Craig, I was still fine. But Brian? Brian had done the work of an army. He'd invaded, bombed, and attacked my life, mercilessly and brutally. Yet through all that, I came out on the other side. He tried to burn me, but I came out and I didn't even smell like smoke! The woman I am today, the woman I have become is a woman I am proud of, a woman I am happy my daughters get to see and draw inspiration from.

EPILOGUE

EPILOGUE

The weight of betrayal is a burden that can break even the strongest of souls. I had given everything to a man I thought I knew, only to realize that I had been living a lie. His death was the beginning of a painful journey of discovering the truth about him, piece by piece. Every revelation was like a punch to the gut, each lie more unbelievable than the last. It was a masterful performance of deceit, and I was the unwilling audience. The fallout from his deception was catastrophic. My mental health suffered, and I lost my job, my financial stability, and my peace of mind. It was a never-ending rainstorm, and all my carefully saved funds were washed away in an instant. But I refused to let Brian's actions define me. I fought tooth and nail to clear my name and settle his debts, and finally, I emerged victorious.

Selling the house and getting rid of Brian's belongings was not an easy task. Every item had a story attached to it, and memories of the life we had shared together, but as I went through his things, I realized that the man I thought I knew was not the person I had been living with. His belongings held secrets and lies, and each one was a reminder of the betrayal I had experienced.

I sold the house, the remnants of a life I no longer recognized. With each item I sold, I regained a bit of my power, a bit of my autonomy. I was no longer the victim but the victor, having survived a storm that could have easily destroyed me. The process of selling the house was also emotional. It had been our home, and the place where we had planned our future together. But it was also the place where Brian's lies had taken root, and where he had plotted his deception. Selling it felt like cutting off a part of my past, but it was also the first step towards my future.

The sale of the house was long and complicated, with many legal hurdles to overcome. But in the end, it was worth it. The proceeds of the sale helped me recover some of the legal fees I had paid and it also gave me the financial freedom to start over. It was a fresh start, a chance to build a new life free from the shadows of his deceit. As I sold off his belongings, I felt a sense of relief. It was as if each item that left my possession was a weight lifted from my shoulders. I sold everything from his clothes to his tools, and each sale felt like a small victory. It was as if I were shedding the last remnants of the life we had shared and making room for a new chapter in my life.

EPILOGUE

In the end, selling the house and his belongings was a cathartic experience. It was a way of letting go of the past and moving forward. It allowed me to reclaim my power and regain control over my life. I may have been broken, but I was also strong enough to pick up the pieces and rebuild myself into the person I wanted to be. And now, I use my experience to protect my children, to warn them of the dangers of falling for the wrong person.

I am *beautifully* broken. I have been shattered, but I have also been rebuilt, stronger and wiser than before. Brian may have thought he had won, but in the end, it was I, who emerged victorious. The mask he wore has been shattered, revealing the true face of a man I never truly knew. But I have found my own true self in the aftermath, and I am ready to face whatever comes my way with renewed strength and resilience. *It's a New Dawn.*

"Broken Pieces" is a gripping and emotionally charged novel that delves into the life of a woman who falls head over heels for what seems like the perfect man, only to have her dreams shattered when she uncovers a web of deceit. This book takes readers on a journey of love, loss, and Self-discovery. Paula, the protagonist, is a vibrant and independent woman who believes she has finally found her soulmate in Brian, a charming and charismatic man. They share a deep connection, and Paula quickly falls in love, blissfully unaware of the dark secrets that lie beneath Brian's charming exterior. The once seemingly perfect love story is revealed to be a facade, leaving Paula to pick up the shattered pieces of her life and find the strength to move forward. Throughout the book she relies on the support, friendship, and wisdom of her loyal best friend who stands by her side through thick and thin.

Printed in the USA
CPSIA information can be obtained
at www.ICGtesting.com
LVHW020935241023
761969LV00009B/59